EYE ON ART

Graffiti

Vandalism or Art?

By Anna Collins

Portions of this book originally appeared in *Graffiti* by Michael V. Uschan.

LUCENT
PRESS

Published in 2018 by
Lucent Press, an Imprint of Greenhaven Publishing, LLC
353 3rd Avenue
Suite 255
New York, NY 10010

Designer: Seth Hughes
Editor: Jennifer Lombardo

Library of Congress Cataloging-in-Publication Data

Names: Collins, Anna, author.
Title: Graffiti : vandalism or art? / Anna Collins.
Description: New York : Lucent Press, 2018. | Series: Eye on art | Includes bibliographical references and index.
Identifiers: LCCN 2017017076 | ISBN 9781534561120 (library bound book)
Subjects: LCSH: Graffiti. | Street art.
Classification: LCC GT3912 .C65 2018 | DDC 751.7/3–dc23
LC record available at https://lccn.loc.gov/2017017076

Printed in the United States of America

CPSIA compliance information: Batch #BS17KL: For further information contact Greenhaven Publishing LLC, New York, New York at 1-844-317-7404.

Please visit our website, www.greenhavenpublishing.com. For a free color catalog of all our high-quality books, call toll free 1-844-317-7404 or fax 1-844-317-7405.

Contents

Foreword

When many people think of art, the first things that come to mind may be paintings, drawings, sculptures, or even pictures created entirely with a computer. However, people have been applying artistic elements to almost every aspect of life for thousands of years. Human beings love beautiful things, and they seek beauty in unlikely places. Buildings, clothes, furniture, and many other things we use every day can all have an artistic aspect to them.

Attempts to define art have frequently fallen short. Merriam-Webster defines art as "something that is created with imagination and skill and that is beautiful or that expresses important ideas or feelings." However, almost no one refers to the dictionary definition when attempting to decide whether or not something can be considered art. They rely on their intuition, which leaves much room for debate between competing opinions. What one person views as beautiful, another may see as ugly. An idea that an artist feels it is important to express may hit home with some people and be dismissed by others. Some people believe that art should always be beautiful, while others feel that art should be unsettling enough to pull people out of their comfort zone. With all of these contradictory views, it is no wonder that the question of what is art is so often disputed.

This series aims to introduce readers to some of the more unconventional and controversial art forms, such as anime, fashion design, and graffiti. Debate on these topics has often been heated, with some people firmly declaring that they are art and others declaring just as firmly that they are not. Each book in the series discusses the history of a particular art form, the ways it is created, and the reasons why it is considered artistic. Learning more about these topics helps young adults recognize the art that is all around them as well as form their own opinions about this complex subject.

Quotes by experts in various art fields enhance the engaging text. All quotes are cited so readers can trace them back to their original source, giving them a starting point for further research. A list of recommended books and websites also allows young adults to delve deeper into related subjects. Full-color photographs give vivid examples of the artistic works being described in the books so readers can visualize the terms they are learning.

Through this series, young adults gain a better understanding of a variety of popular art forms. They also develop a deeper appreciation for the artistry that is inherent in the things they see and use every day.

INTRODUCTION

Understanding Graffiti

According to Merriam-Webster, the definition of graffiti is "usually unauthorized writing or drawing on a public surface."[1] This makes it different from murals, which are generally commissioned, or ordered, by the property owner. Some people also see a difference between graffiti and street art, although the terms are often used interchangeably, and the definitions of each are the subject of much debate. Generally, "graffiti" is used to describe a work that is done illegally, while "street art" is typically used to describe a work that has been done with the property owner's permission. However, some people use the word "graffiti" to describe a particular style of art, whether or not it is done illegally.

Graffiti is a complex subject, one that many people have trouble understanding. Even the word itself is confusing. "Graffiti" is the plural form of *graffito*, a word that refers to one example of anything that meets the above definition. However, the word "graffiti" is also a mass noun (a noun that refers to things that cannot be counted, such as freedom or honesty), and it can be used in the singular. Further complicating the term are the various types of graffiti. Several varieties of graffiti are swear words or gang names scrawled on walls or other flat surfaces, which most people consider vandalism. Graffiti, however, can be more than an act of public vandalism. It is also a distinctive art form, one which

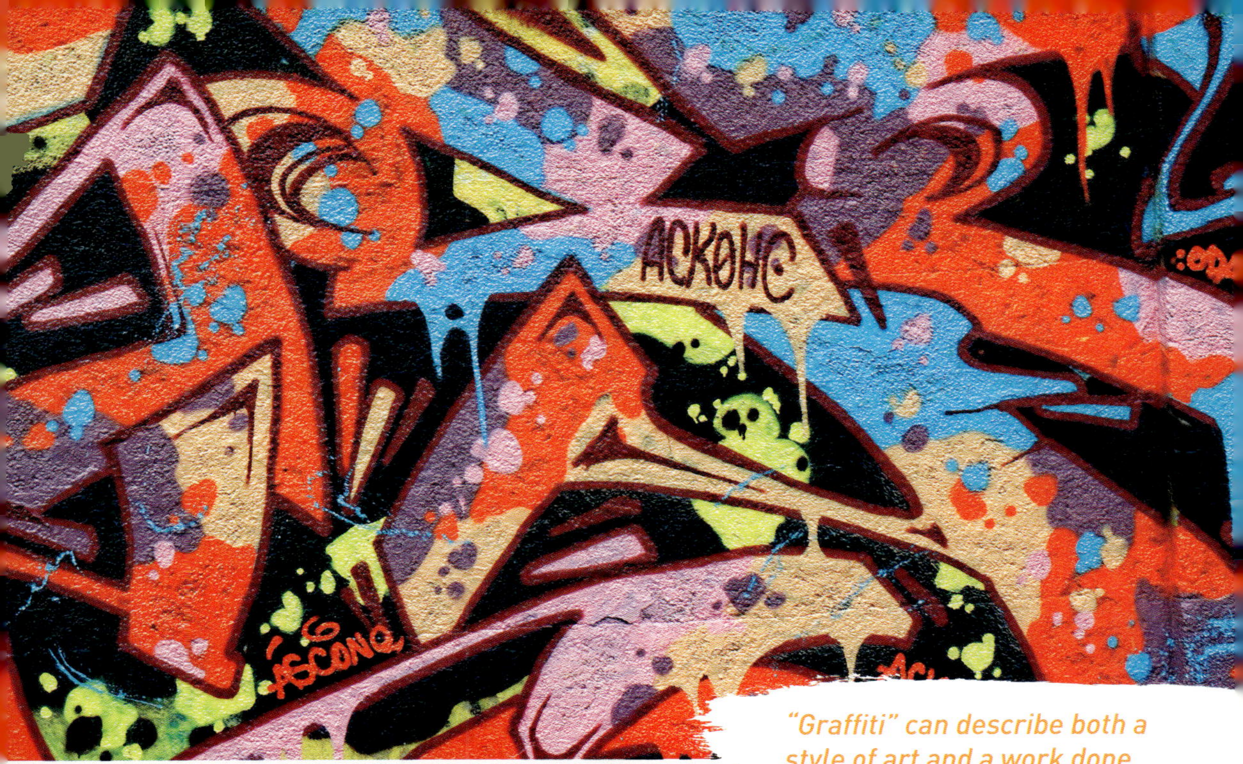

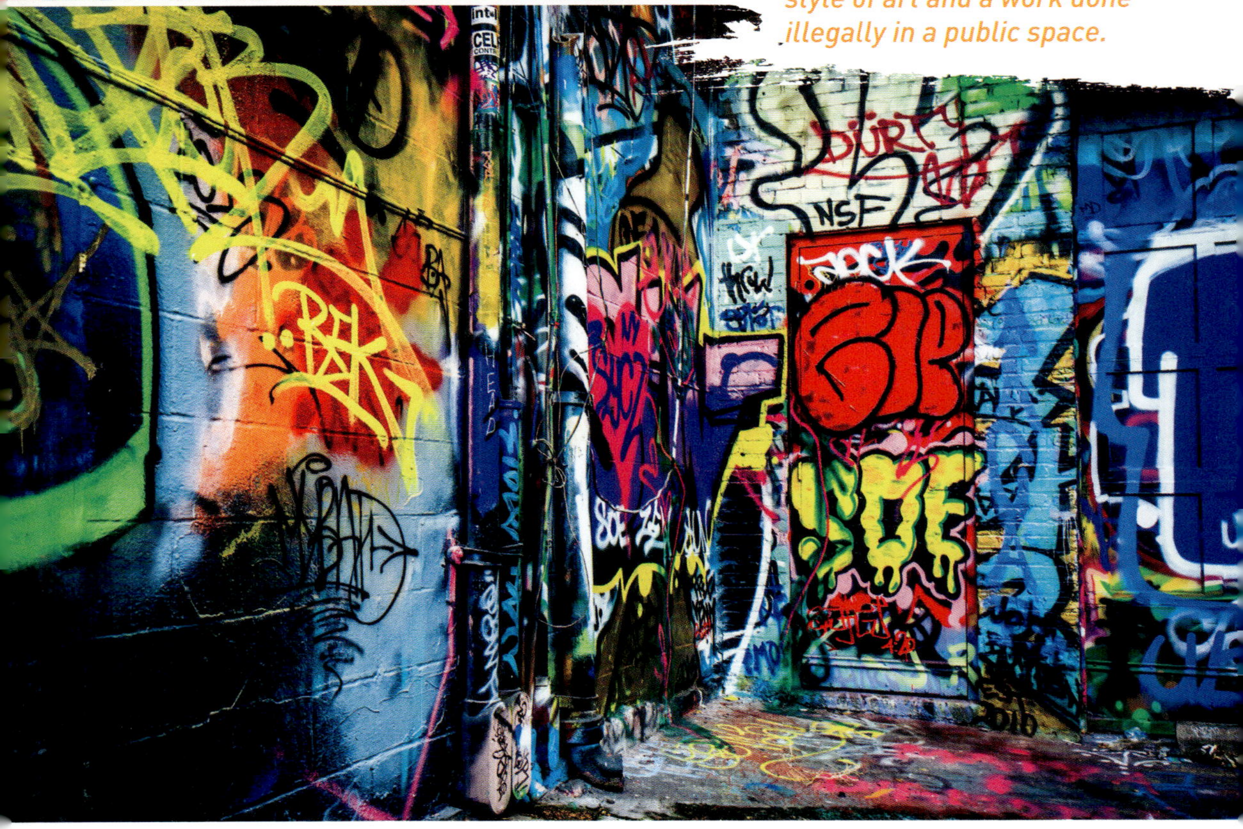

"Graffiti" can describe both a style of art and a work done illegally in a public space.

graffiti artists cherish and believe other people should respect even if they do not understand or like it. However, even when it is considered art, any painting that is done without the property owner's permission is considered an illegal activity, which is why most graffiti is done at night or when no one else is around.

Although the act of graffiti is often performed in secret, some graffiti artists are well known. Scape Martinez is a San Jose, California, artist who became famous by adorning hundreds, perhaps thousands, of walls with his distinctive tag. "Tag" is the term graffiti artists use for the elaborate signatures they place on walls and other public areas. Martinez has created murals and other works that have been shown in prestigious art galleries, but he still admires graffiti. Martinez believes graffiti is "a uniquely American art form" and claims its power stems from the fact that it is displayed publicly so that many people can see and be touched by it. He wrote, "[Graffiti] is a visual narrative [that] directly connects the street corner to the spirit, bypassing the definitions of art presented by art galleries and museums."[2] Today, Martinez hosts workshops to teach young adults the art of graffiti.

However, Martinez was only partially correct when he wrote that graffiti is an American art form. Although colorful graffiti did originate in the United States, other forms of graffiti existed for thousands of years before the country was created.

The Evolution of Graffiti

From the beginning of written language until the late 20th century, graffiti consisted mainly of words, often no more than someone's name. People sometimes added small drawings, some of them as beautiful as any traditional art created at the time. However, in the late 1960s and early 1970s, a new style of graffiti appeared in New York City that was much more creative, vibrant, and noticeable. Young people, mostly from poor black and Latinx neighborhoods, began creating elaborate, multicolored copies of their tags. Most tags were done in spray paint and appeared on the sides of buildings, bridges, and other flat surfaces. Graffiti artists even began tagging subway cars and buses, which became giant mobile works of art that were viewed by millions of people as they traveled through major cities.

The artists who initiated the modern graffiti that is still popular today referred to themselves as "writers" even though their work was far more artistic than mere printed letters. Unlike previous graffiti, the words splashed on various surfaces with markers and spray paint were not written in simple letters. Instead, these tags, along with the symbols and cartoons that sometimes accompanied them, were artistically and whimsically designed.

The motivation graffiti artists had was the same one that led early people to cover walls with primitive paintings—a desire to

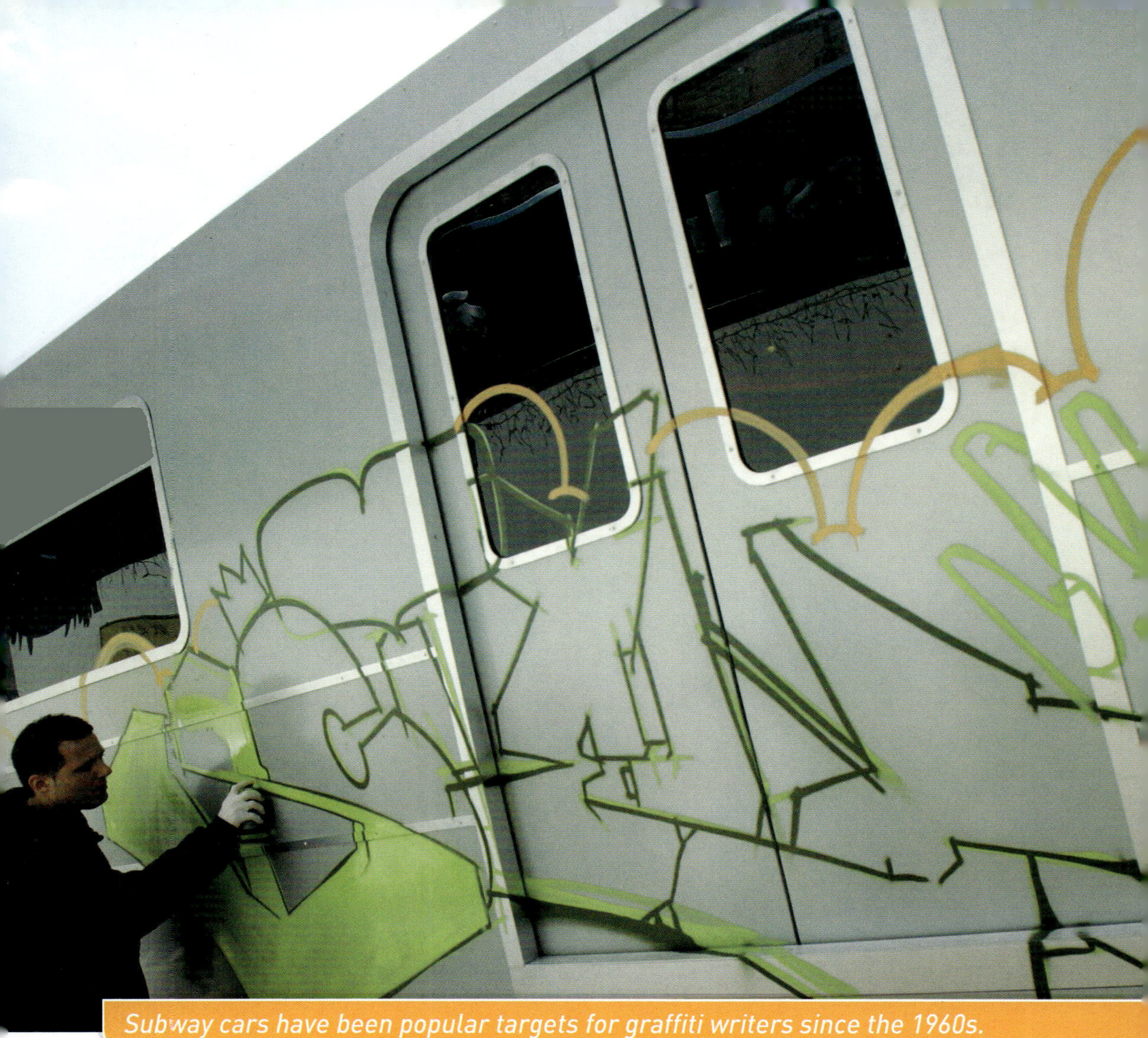

Subway cars have been popular targets for graffiti writers since the 1960s.

communicate with other people and leave a record of their existence. Author Stephen Powers explained this need in his book *The Art of Getting Over: Graffiti at the Millennium*. He wrote,

> *If you've ever walked down the street, seen a name, and wondered what that marking meant, I'll tell you: It means somebody is telling you a story about who they are and what they are prepared to do to make you aware of it. Every time a name is written, a story gets told. It's a short story: "I was here."*[3]

Despite the efforts of graffiti artists to make themselves known, the names they plaster on walls, buildings, and subway cars are often not their real names. They use street aliases because they know they are doing something illegal.

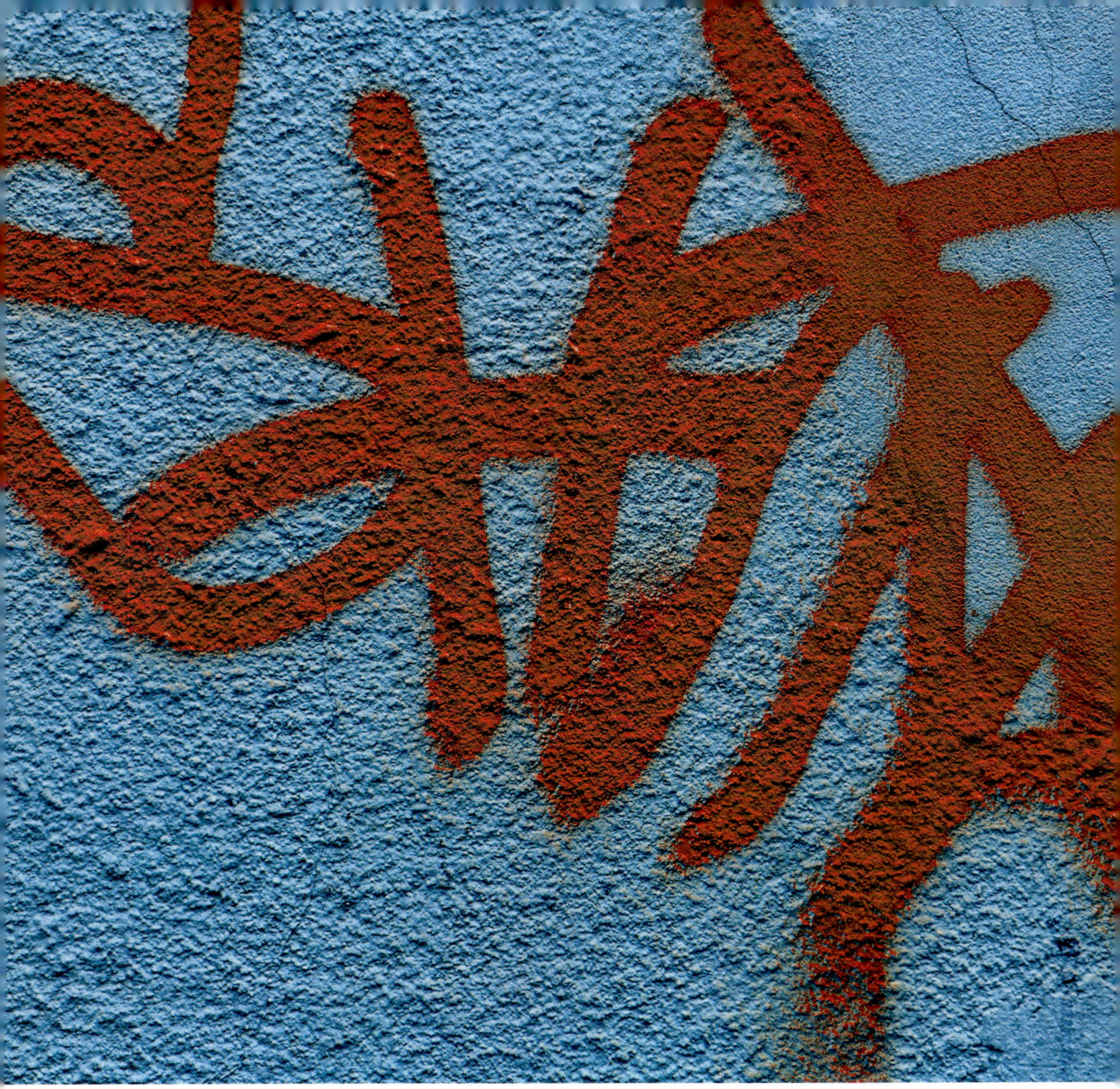

Eyesore or Art?

When modern graffiti began emerging in the 1960s and 1970s, public officials, businesspeople, and civic leaders routinely condemned it because the artists never asked permission to use the public spaces that became canvases for their work. Graffiti artists were considered trespassers on public and private property, and their work was labeled vandalism instead of art. An editorial in a Philadelphia, Pennsylvania, newspaper on May 20, 1974, condemned graffiti: "Despite what some advanced thinkers suggest is a new art form, graffiti in its mindless scrawls on city walls is ugly, ugly, ugly. These idiotic and sleazy scrawls

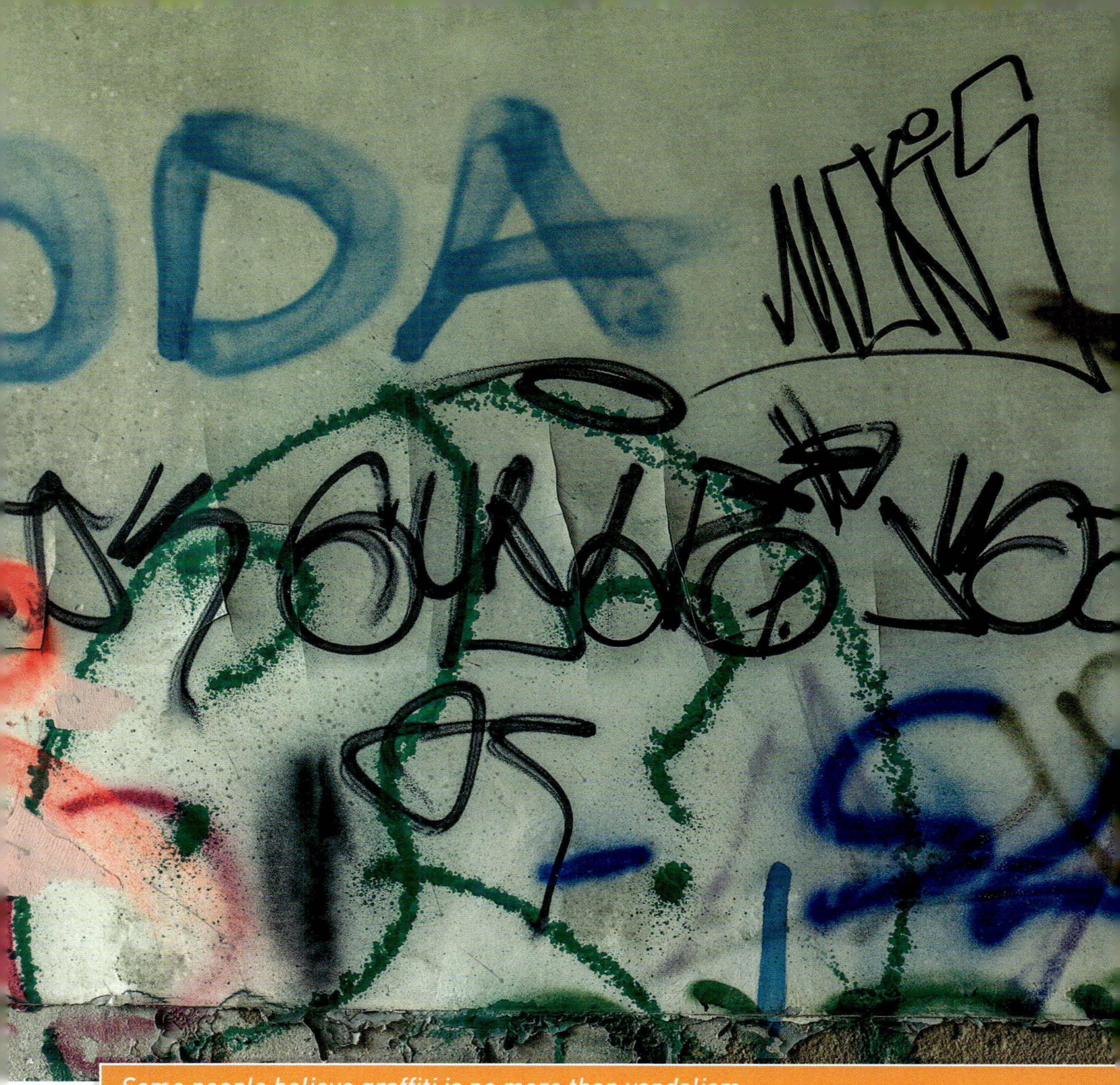

Some people believe graffiti is no more than vandalism.

are criminal and have to be treated as such."[4]

The article summed up the negative attitudes many people had toward graffiti—it was vandalism that was an eyesore and a nuisance, and it was expensive to remove from surfaces that had been illegally decorated. This attitude toward graffiti still prevails today for the same reasons, even though some artists now work only on spaces for which they have permission. However, despite the negatives, modern graffiti developed into a powerful form of creative expression that grew in popularity in the United States and has since spread around the world.

CHAPTER ONE

Graffiti Through the Years

Spray paint is a relatively new creation, but people have been finding ways to leave their mark for centuries. Early people created a paint-like mixture by combining their saliva with red ochre, a brown or red pigment, or color, that occurs naturally in clay. Later, people also used sharp objects to carve messages into wood and sometimes even stone.

Although some graffiti today has an artistic element, most early graffiti was intended simply to leave a message in the most straightforward way possible. Cave paintings were a way for people to communicate before written language. Ancient Roman and Egyptian graffiti gave people a way to express their philosophical ideas, show disapproval of political decisions, and leave evidence of their personalities. Today, graffiti is used in much the same way. Some works are simple tags that people use to mark an area as their own. Others use combinations of words and symbolic pictures to send political messages or show disapproval of something, such as capitalism or war. The only thing that has changed with time is the style of the graffiti.

Rock Art

Prehistoric art is commonly referred to as rock art because the art was often created on, or made from, rock that has survived to modern times. Although millions of rock-art sites are scattered across the globe, they are mainly found in Africa, Australia, and Europe. The art that has survived for millennia shows

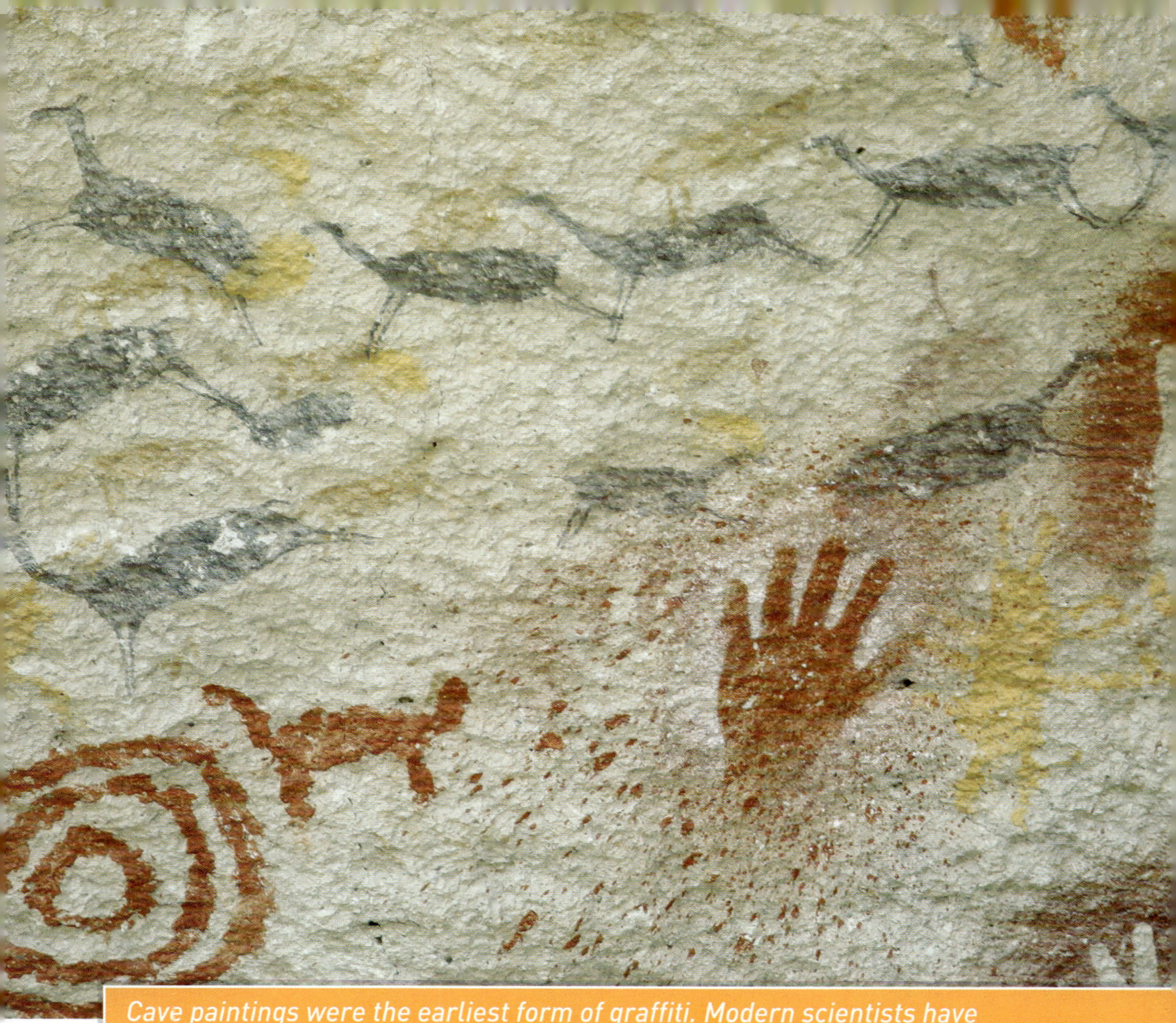

Cave paintings were the earliest form of graffiti. Modern scientists have determined that many of them were done by teenage boys.

images ranging from geometric designs and unidentified abstract symbols to scenes of people and animals. These images were either scratched into rock with crude tools, such as animal bones, or painted with simple pigments or even blood.

Studies of cave art have revealed that while some works were done by expert artists, many others were done by teenage boys:

Men and women have different hand proportions—men have thicker thumbs and palms—so by analyzing the dimensions of the hands in European cave art, and comparing them to 1,000 photocopies of modern hands of men and women of different ages, [paleobiologist Dale] Guthrie determined just who painted what.

Men and women and boys and girls of all ages left their marks but, statistically, teenage males dominated, contrary to popular belief.[5]

In December 1994, one of the most famous collections of prehistoric art was discovered in southeast France. The Chauvet-Pont-d'Arc cave is notable because some of the hundreds of drawings that cover its walls include animals that today are found only in Africa and had never been portrayed in previously found European rock art. Additionally, carbon dating—a way for experts to determine the age of historical items—showed that the oldest drawings in the cave were more than twice as old as previous cave art finds, which changed researchers' estimates about when humans first began creating art.

The art in the Chauvet cave is well preserved because it is inside, which protects it from the elements. In 2015, a replica cave was opened nearby so people could view copies of the paintings without running the risk of damaging them. However, most prehistoric art sites have been found in open-air spaces—just as graffiti is generally found in public spaces so other people can see it—where wind and water have combined over the centuries to destroy much of the original art.

For thousands of years, such simple drawings were the only way people could leave a lasting imprint of their thoughts and feelings. Gradually, however, humans learned how to communicate through writing.

Communicating Through Symbols

The need to communicate complex ideas to others forced people thousands of years ago to invent written languages and numeric systems. The earliest forms of writing consisted of pictographs, symbols that expressed words or ideas. Many ancient examples of pictographs and petroglyphs—a pictograph drawn or carved on rock—exist today because they were carved on substances durable enough to survive for thousands of years, such as whale tusks, animal bones, animal skins, and tree bark.

Archaeologist Rodney S. Young studied pictographs inscribed 32,000 years ago on limestone walls in Turkey. He said the pictographs might look like aimless doodling, but they are important historical records of daily life in that long-ago era. He wrote, "These drawings are the products not of specialists, but of common citizens; they reflect the contemporary scene, the things which the common man saw about him as he circulated every day. [They] are important sources for the life of the time—contemporary illustrations from a world long forgotten."[6]

Some pictographs are huge, such as the Nazca Lines in Peru. The Nazca geoglyphs—the name for pictographs carved into the ground—are more than 2,500 years old. People of the Nazca culture made them by removing surface rock to reveal white-colored ground underneath. The figures include artistic representations of monkeys, sharks, and

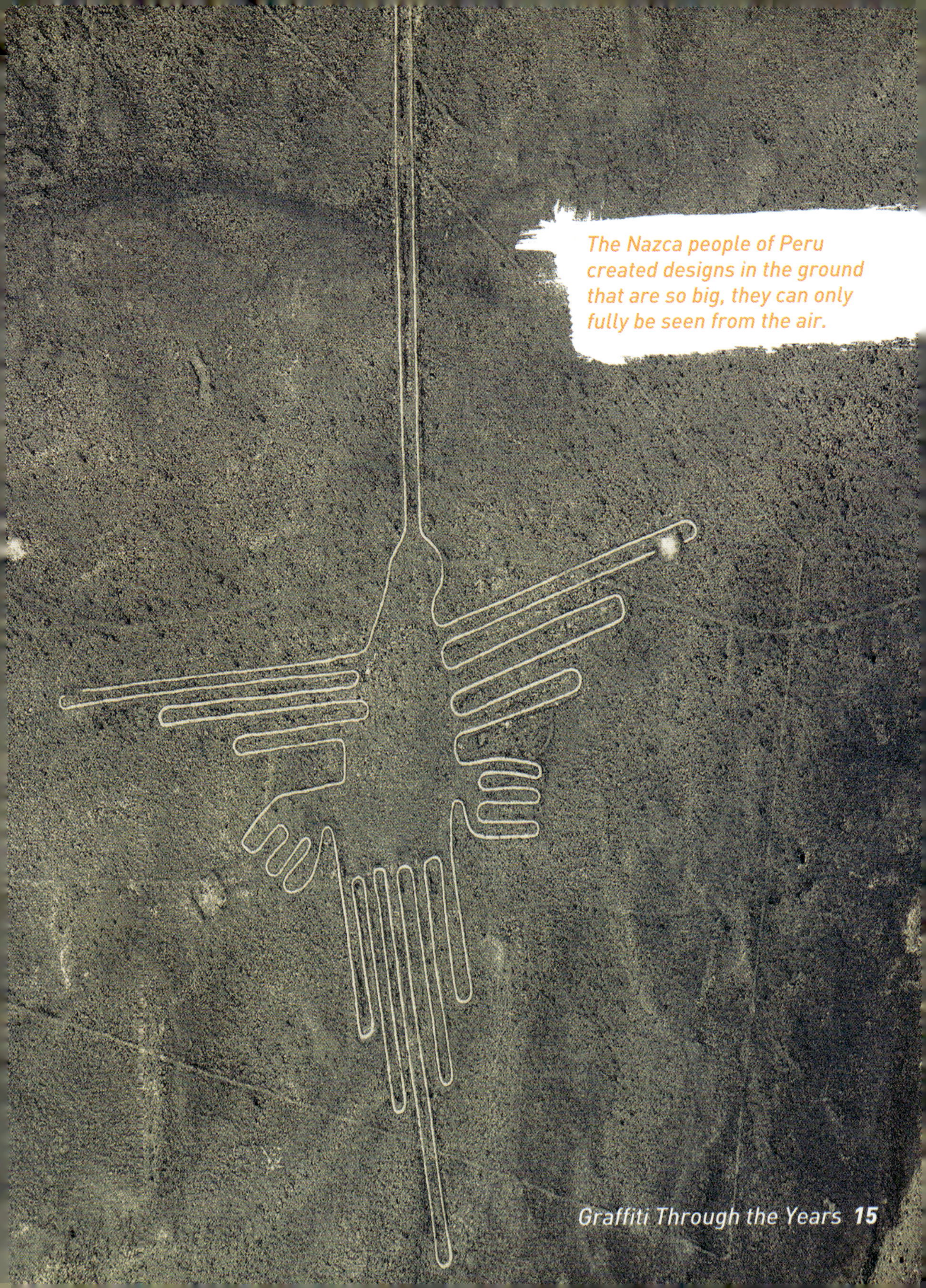

The Nazca people of Peru created designs in the ground that are so big, they can only fully be seen from the air.

llamas, and the largest are more than 660 feet (201 m) wide.

Over the centuries, people invented alphabets so they could write words. Written language changed graffiti by allowing individuals to communicate advanced ideas with one another more easily than they could with symbols. Once written language was available, most graffiti used words rather than pictures.

Communicating with Words

Some surviving samples of graffiti writing are more than 2,000 years old. Written words found scratched on rocks and boulders in the desert of southern Syria, eastern Jordan, and northern Saudi Arabia date from about 100 BC. They are historically important because they are the only existing remnants of Safaitic, an early form of Arabic writing. Ancient writings from Egypt, Greece, and the Roman Empire also have survived because they were etched or engraved into stone or wood.

The largest collection of ancient graffiti exists in Rome, Italy. More than 500,000 examples of it were found in the Roman catacombs—underground burial places beneath Rome that were used mainly by early Christians. The messages etched into the catacomb walls between the fourth and seventh centuries include comments from a variety of writers, ranging from gladiators to young children.

Archaeologists found another valuable collection of graffiti when they

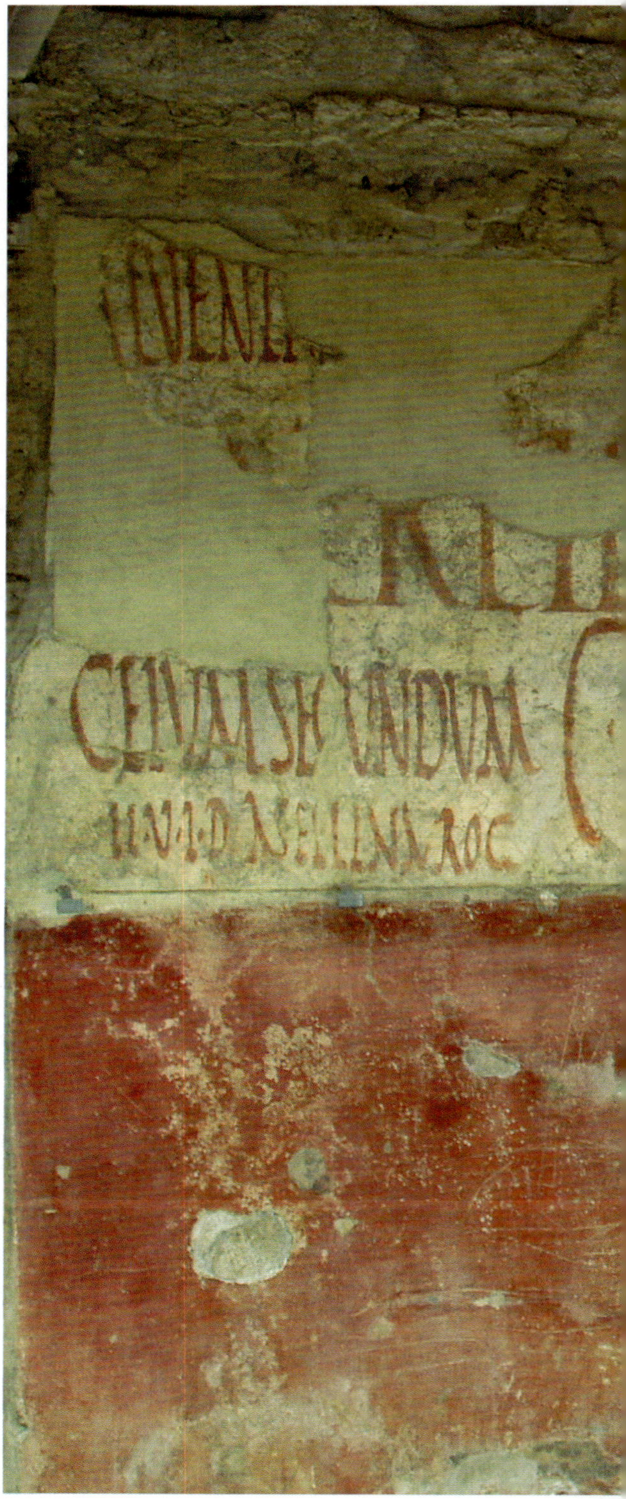

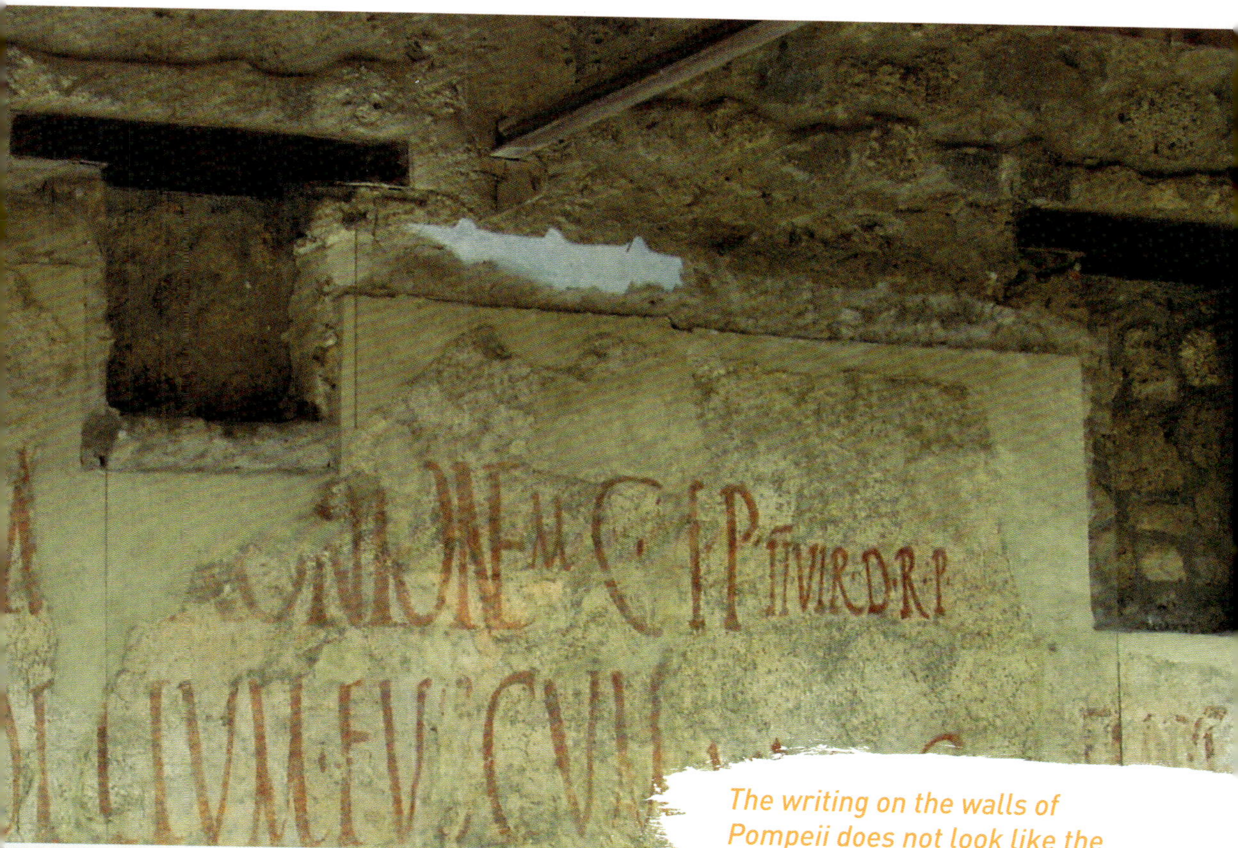

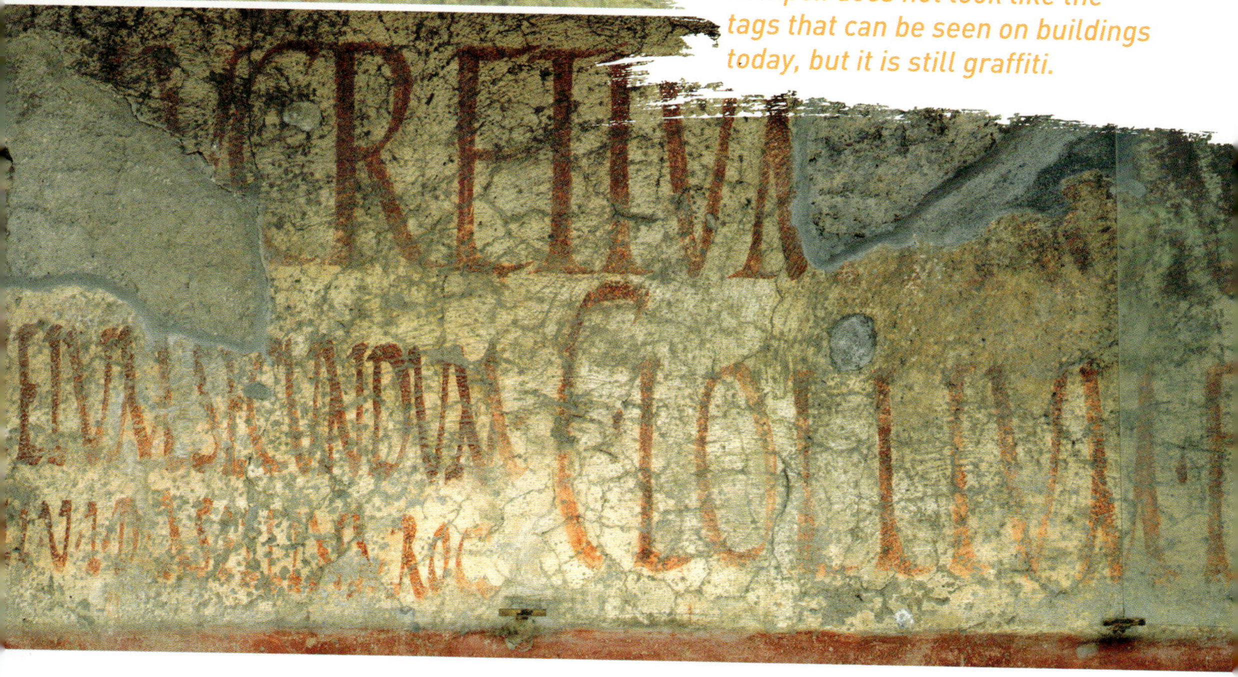

The writing on the walls of Pompeii does not look like the tags that can be seen on buildings today, but it is still graffiti.

excavated Pompeii, an Italian city that was buried under mountains of ash and cinder after the volcanic eruption of Mount Vesuvius in AD 79. Many people were surprised to find that the messages people wrote on walls at that time were similar to the ones people scratch into surfaces today. Some were simple messages such as *Lucius pinxit*, Latin for "Lucius painted this," while others were insults about other people, such as *Oppi, emboliari, fur, furuncle*, which translates to, "Oppius, you're a clown, a thief, and a cheap crook." Some of the messages were crude and mentioned bodily functions. These showed researchers that human nature has not changed much over the centuries.

During the Middle Ages, which spanned from from roughly the 5th to the 15th centuries, it was popular in England to engrave graffiti on churches. Many inscriptions were in Latin, and they often contained expressions of religiousness such as this statement etched on St. Mary's Church in Ashwell: "The end of virtue is God's glory and not the merit of the virtuous one." People used chisels or sharpened styluses to carve and scrape their remarks and sometimes added small drawings. Historian Violet Pritchard believed that people who created the flowing script of such messages and artwork were as skilled as any artists of their period. She noted that "owing to the constant cleaning and scraping of the stone surface [over centuries, some] graffiti only show the deeper part of the incision and much of their original beauty and craftsmanship has thus been lost."[7]

What Is Vandalism?

Some people argue that the dictionary definition of "vandalism" is open to interpretation. Merriam-Webster defines vandalism as "willful or malicious destruction or defacement of public or private property."[1] This can mean any kind of drawings or markings on public property. However, some people argue that certain instances of graffiti should not be considered vandalism. For instance, some believe graffiti that is clever or beautiful is a worthwhile addition to buildings, street signs, and other public items. Everyone's definition of "clever" or "beautiful" is subjective—people view things differently based on their values and past experiences. However, even when people enjoy a particular piece of graffiti, it is still legally considered vandalism if it was done without permission. For this reason, people who oppose all forms of crime often consider all works of graffiti to be vandalism.

1. *Merriam-Webster Online*, s.v. "vandalism," accessed May 15, 2017. www.merriam-webster.com/dictionary/vandalism.

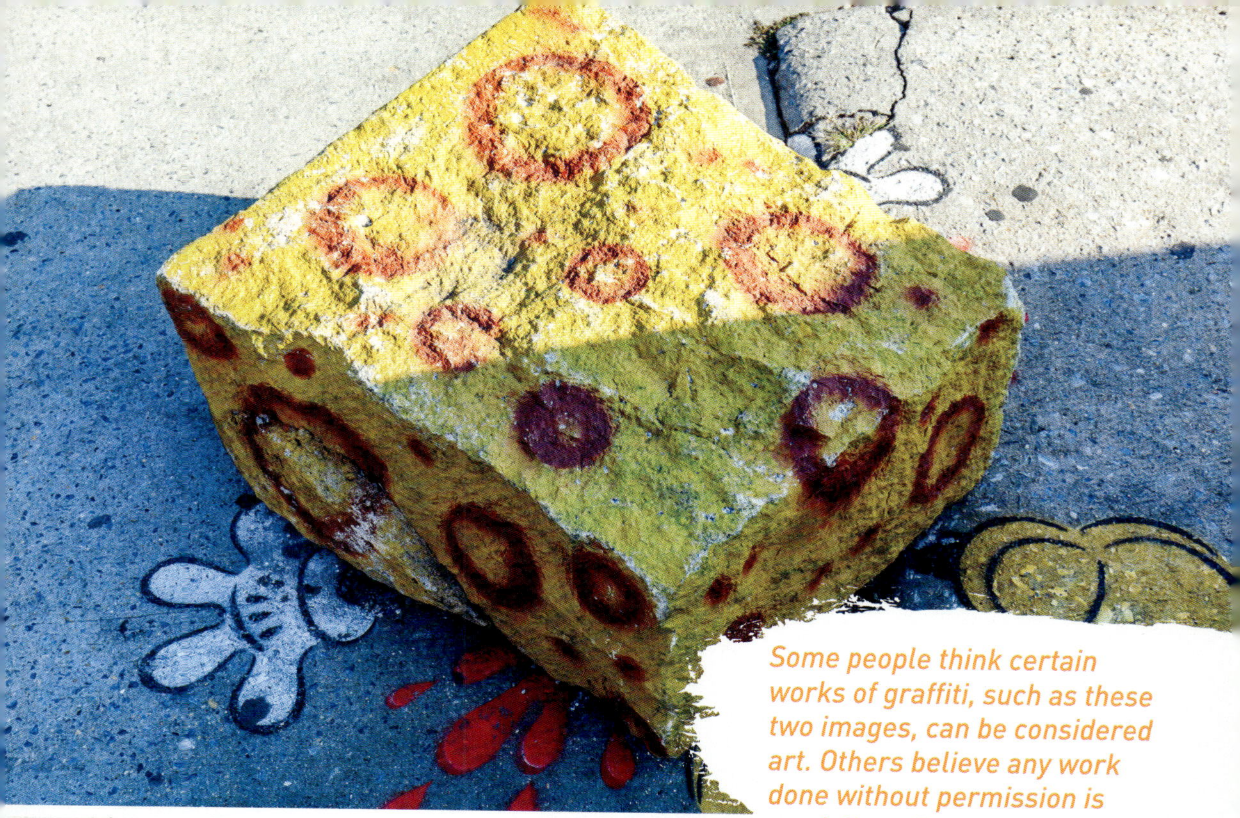

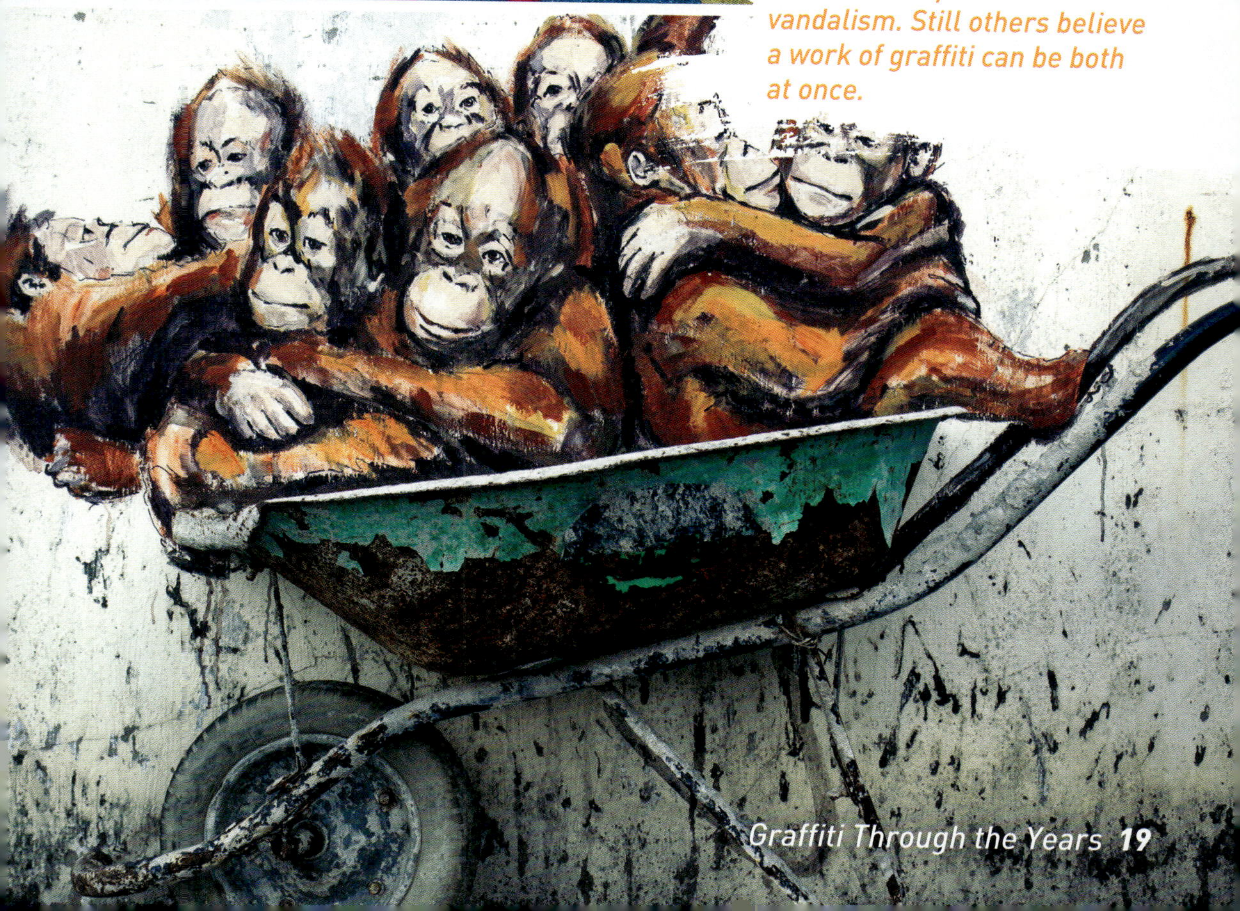

Some people think certain works of graffiti, such as these two images, can be considered art. Others believe any work done without permission is vandalism. Still others believe a work of graffiti can be both at once.

Marking Gang Territory

Some of the most common 20th-century graffiti in the United States has been done by street gangs in big cities. This has led many people to associate graffiti with gang activity, which is one reason why it has often been considered vandalism more than art.

As early as the 1930s, Latinx gangs in California were using graffiti to claim possession of neighborhoods. Gang graffiti has continued to flourish in inner-city areas of big cities across the country. According to the late art and graffiti historian Jack Stewart, gangs use the written form to threaten and intimidate other people. He wrote, "[The graffiti] marked the boundaries of their turf; these warnings clearly came from the entire gang, not just from the individual writer."[8] According to the Los Angeles Police Department, gang graffiti is dangerous because it "is meant to create a sense of intimidation and may increase the sense of fear within a neighborhood ... When a neighborhood is marked with graffiti indicating territorial dominance, the entire area and its inhabitants become targets for violence."[9]

Most gang graffiti is written simply, although gangs will often write their name in an elaborate style of large letters that are referred to as *placas*, which use an Old English style that has looped, pointed, and boxed or squared letters. Such graffiti often includes the name of the gang and its individual members along with gang symbols or numbers identifying the gang.

Everyday Graffiti

Most written graffiti is not threatening; in fact, it is often humorous or silly. For instance, an apparently irritated student once wrote this inscription on a wall at the Harvard University library: "I've decided that to raise my grades I must lower my standards."[10]

Graffiti appears on all kinds of surfaces: trees, walls, posters, street signs, and more. So many messages have been written in public bathrooms that this graffiti genre has its own name—latrinalia. The term was coined in 1996 by Alan Dundes, a former professor of folklore and anthropology at the University of California, Berkeley. Experts have studied these bathroom messages and found that there are certain differences between the latrinalia most often written by men and women. Men tend to write simple declarations (for instance, "Mike was here"), as well as statements that are aggressive or sexual. In contrast, women tend to write insults about others and statements about love. Researchers believe these differences are not due to biological differences between men and women, but to their surroundings in gender-segregated bathrooms. According to *The Atlantic*,

> *When you write on a bathroom wall, "you have a staggeringly diverse audience," [Nicholas Matthews, a PhD candidate at Indiana University,] points out. "Many different races, classes, all walks of life, but it's completely confined to*

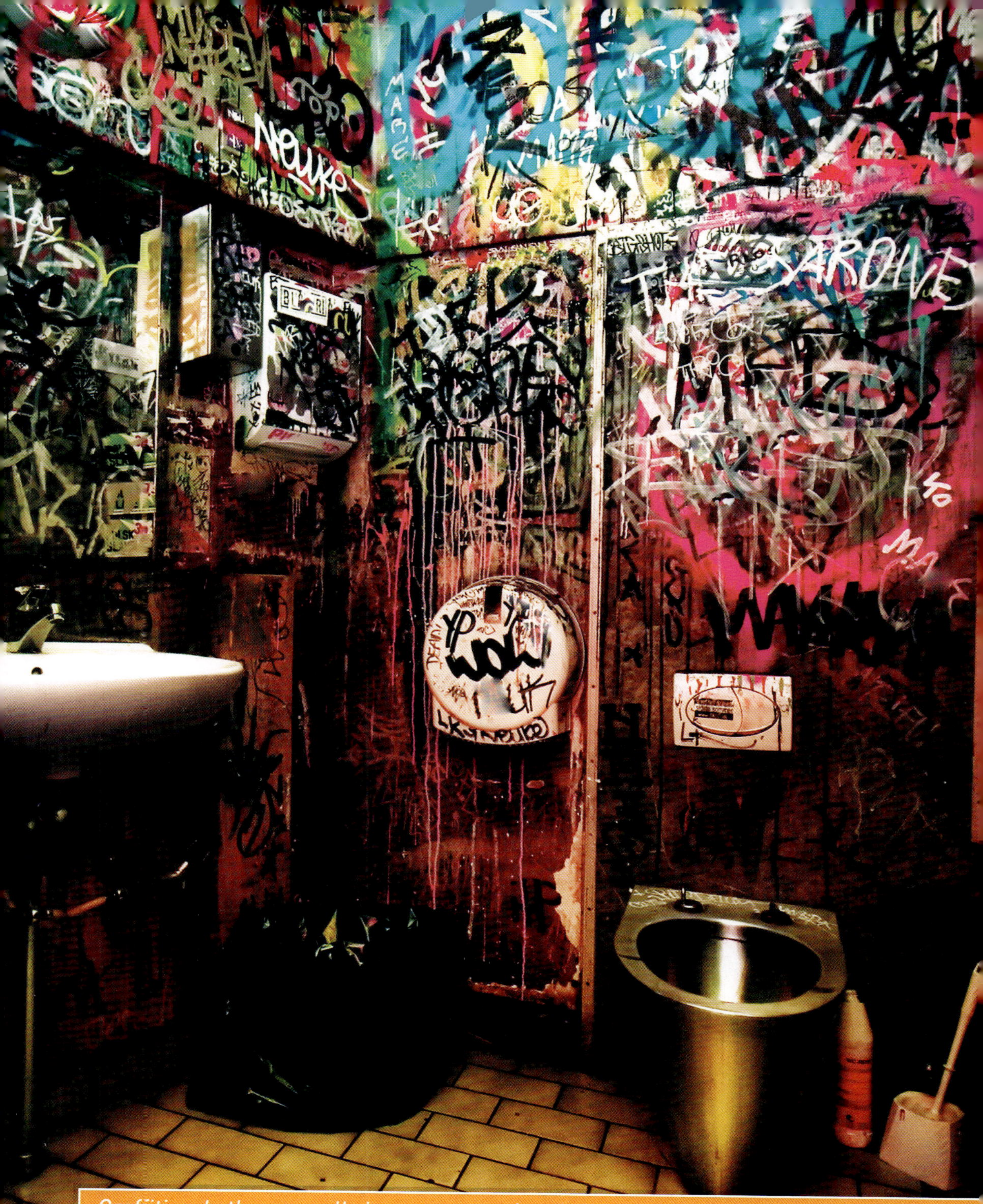

Graffiti on bathroom walls is so common that the word latrinalia *was invented to define it.*

a single gender. So it suddenly lets gender-specific issues emerge."

Bathroom graffiti artists have a "captive audience," [psychology professor Nick] Haslam notes, for whatever issues may be on their minds. "There's a space, there's some time on your hands, and people love to communicate. We're social creatures. A tradition grew up of people doing this."[11]

Leaving a Mark

People throughout recorded history have used graffiti as a way to mark where they have been. For example, when French soldiers invaded Egypt in 1798, they scrawled their names on the great pyramids of Egypt to prove

Graffiti and Musicians

People often write graffiti in places that have emotional importance to them, such as sites that are connected with their favorite artists. The Beatles were one of the most famous bands in history, and they released the album *Abbey Road* in 1969. This is the name of a street in London, England, and the location of Abbey Road Studios, where the band recorded most of their albums. For years, Beatles fans have been signing the wall outside the recording studio with names, dates, and messages of peace and love.

Graceland is the home rock-and-roll icon Elvis Presley lived in until he died on August 16, 1977. This Memphis, Tennessee, home is now a popular tourist attraction for his fans, and one way they honor him is by writing graffiti on a wall there. Author Daniel Wright explained,

> *While Elvis was alive, the groundskeepers did their best to keep the wall clean. After his death, however, the sheer volume of the graffiti proved overwhelming, and officials with the estate decided to leave the wall alone. ... Today, writing on the wall is as much a part of the Graceland experience as seeing the Jungle Room and the grave site. The wall is so long that you could spend hours reading from one end to the other. As you read, you'll likely see several tourists with markers in hand stopping to add their messages or have their snapshots taken next to a memorable piece of graffiti. Celebrities in town for a film or concert often pay tribute on the wall including rocker Billy Idol, who painted "Long live the King" in huge red letters.*[1]

1. Daniel Wright, *Dear Elvis: Graffiti from Graceland*. Memphis, TN: Mustang, 1996, pp. 38–39.

they had visited the famous historical landmarks. The United States has an especially rich history of travel graffiti. For several hundred years explorers, fur trappers, and settlers moving westward across the continent left personalized messages of their passage.

El Morro National Monument in New Mexico contains some of the nation's oldest graffiti. *El Morro* is a Spanish name—in English it means "the headland"—because it was named by Spanish explorers such as Juan de Oñate. Like hundreds of U.S. soldiers, miners, and settlers who would follow him, Oñate, in 1605, signed his name on the huge sandstone wall and wrote, "pasa por aqui" (passed by here). In 1859, P. Gilmer Breckinridge chiseled his name into the same stone bluff after arriving with 25 camels in a failed U.S. Army experiment to use camels for desert travel. Other inscriptions on the bluff at El Morro include those of settlers moving west and workers who built the Union Pacific railroad in the 1860s. However, all of those visitors, including Oñate, were latecomers to the sandstone bluffs, which already had some drawings left hundreds of years earlier by Native American groups such as the Ancestral Puebloans.

In the 19th century, Independence Rock near Casper, Wyoming, was a major stopping point along the Oregon Trail. It was named by a party of fur trappers who camped there on July 4, 1830, and visitors who came afterward were proud enough that they had reached the famed landmark to carve their names in the large granite rock. Also in Wyoming is Signature Rock, a large sandstone cliff whose graffiti includes directions that helped guide settlers on a section of the trail discovered originally by mountain man Jim Bridger in the mid-19th century.

The Wyoming State Historic Preservation Office website says the graffiti is historically important. It states, "The inscriptions also indicate the route the trail took up the valley of Sage Creek. They are very significant because they substantiate the correct route of the Bridger Trail through an area with limited historic evidence concerning the trail route. The location and authenticity of the inscriptions has been confirmed."[12]

One of history's most famous examples of travel graffiti is a long-lasting World War II joke by U.S. soldiers. During the war, soldiers wrote the phrase "Kilroy Was Here" everywhere they traveled, jokingly saying that it was there before they arrived. The scrawled phrase was often accompanied by a comical drawing of a face with a long nose hanging over what seemed to be a wall. A shipyard worker named James J. Kilroy took credit for the phrase, saying he wrote it on ships he inspected to prove to his crew leader that he had done the work he was assigned. Even before the Internet and social media, the message was one of the first known instances of a viral meme.

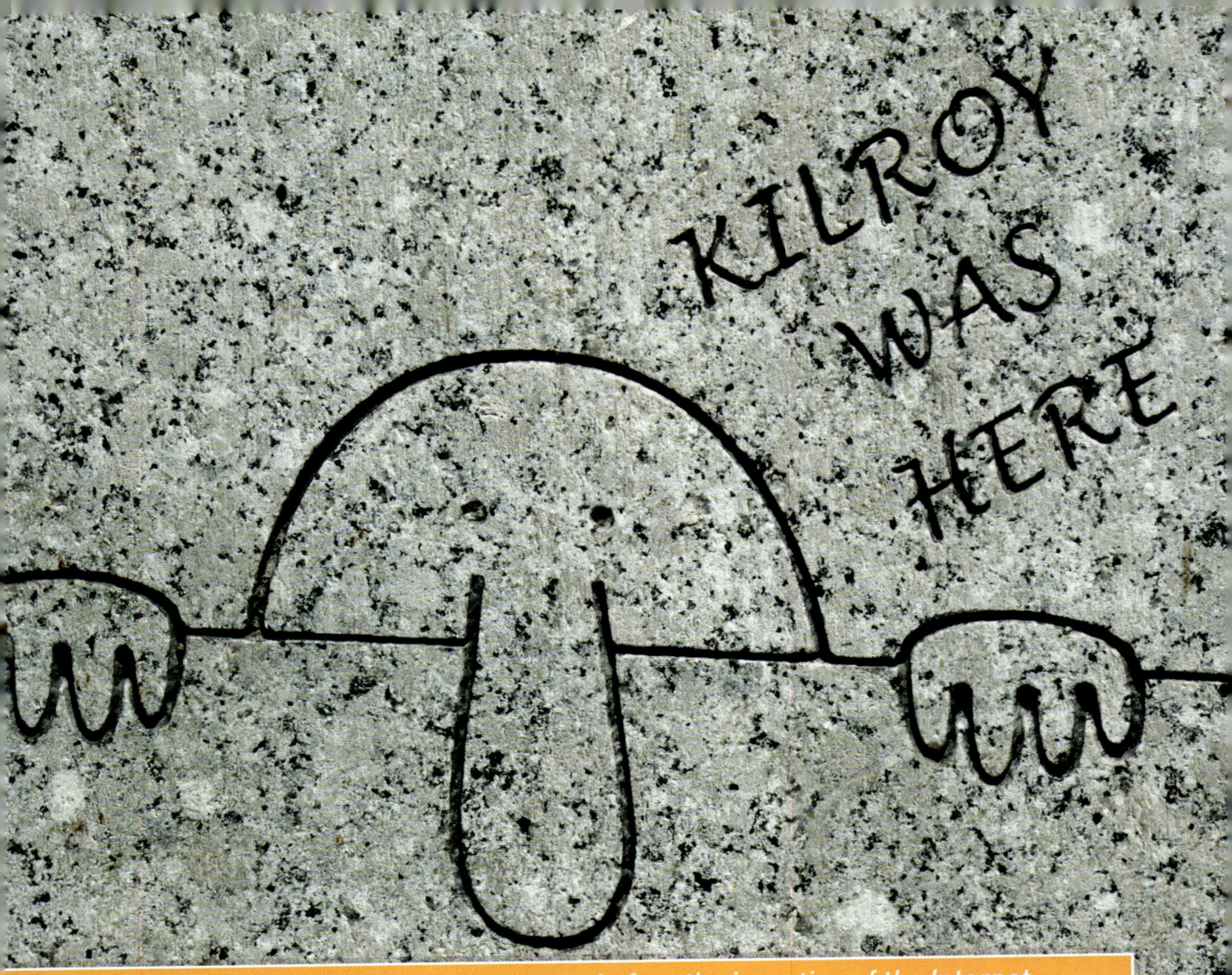

This graffiti became a viral meme even before the invention of the Internet.

Human Nature Stays the Same

Viewing graffiti throughout history gives researchers certain insights into human nature. Although some things change depending on the time and place—for instance, the language or style of the graffiti—most of the messages remain the same. Graffiti is often a way for people to prove their existence by simply writing their names or to pass on jokes and communicate with others. Past graffiti also shows that humans have always found crude things such as bodily fluids amusing. However, graffiti has also always been a way for people to express approval or disapproval of public figures and political decisions. As methods of creating graffiti became more advanced over the years, moving from sharpened sticks to spray paint, artists had the opportunity to express themselves in greater detail. British street artist Banksy once said, "If our civilisation was destroyed, future generations would piece together life in the 21st century using only the scrawlings on our subway walls."[13]

A Secret Code

During the Great Depression, some people traveled from city to city looking for work, generally by illegally catching rides on freight trains. These nomadic people, who were called hobos at the time, had a custom of leaving messages for each other that were written in a private language composed of symbols. These symbols warned other travelers to avoid dangerous places or let them know where people would treat them kindly. For example, a rectangle with a circular dot meant danger, and a circle enclosing a curly line meant that a courthouse or police station was close by. Names, nicknames, or initials were messages similar to modern-day graffiti tags; when they were accompanied by dates and arrows pointing in a particular direction, they let friends know when a person had been in that area and which direction they had gone. Author Robert George Reisner explained,

> *[Nomads] accepted and took care of each other in much the same spirit that members of a religious sect, ethnic group, or respectable fraternity will take care of each other. And the way they did it was through their graffiti. It was a highly imaginative, effectively functional written sign language, conveying important survival information such as the presence of vicious dogs, hostile police officers, areas where handouts could be expected, medical aid secured, or chain gangs existed. Chalked on backyard fences, doorsteps of houses, freight yard buildings, walls of public facilities, ashcans, [and buildings], a great many of the signs were around for [decades]. The graffiti of the hobo are the stationary expression of a mobile group.*[1]

1. Robert George Reisner, *Graffiti: Two Thousand Years of Wall Writing*. Chicago, IL: Regnery, 1971, p. 79.

CHAPTER TWO

A New Type of Graffiti

Graffiti did not change much throughout history until the mid-1960s, when a different style of graffiti began appearing on walls in Philadelphia, Pennsylvania. Spray paint had been invented in 1949 as a way for people to quickly and easily repaint things around their homes, but it quickly became associated with graffiti artists. The *New York Times* explained why spray paint became so widely used by street artists:

> *It came in small, easy-to-conceal, easy-to-steal cans. It was paint and brush in one. It dried quickly. It worked well on building materials and subway cars. More important, perhaps, the imprecise application lent it an inherent disregard. Its inability to be perfectly controlled made it an apt metaphor for rebellion.*[14]

In other words, graffiti artists often enjoyed the fact that their work was not perfect; it was one way of showing how little they cared about society's accepted rules. In the next few decades, this modern form of graffiti became a cultural phenomenon that spread across the globe, giving people a new form of artistic expression.

The Origins of Modern-Day Graffiti

Philadelphia residents in the mid-1960s were already accustomed to gang graffiti, the symbols and names gangs scrawled in public places to mark their territory. However, they were unprepared for the new graffiti that suddenly began appearing on walls, on the sides of buses and trolleys, and on just about any other surface that could be reached. The new graffiti was done in marker or spray paint that spelled out the artist's tag or street identity and sometimes included a small drawing. So many tags appeared on the streets of Philadelphia that people began wondering who the taggers were and why they kept putting up these elaborate tags in so many different places.

One of the earliest Philadelphia tags was "CornBread," which was sometimes drawn with a small crown over the name. Many present and past graffiti artists have kept their real names secret, either because they do not want publicity or are still afraid of being charged as criminals for their work. However, Darryl McCray, who is considered one of the fathers of modern graffiti, has admitted he is CornBread. His tag comes from a nickname he earned in a juvenile detention center for begging a cook to make cornbread, a food he loves. In 1967, when McCray was 14 years old, he began writing "CornBread" in his neighborhood to gain the attention of a girl he liked. He wrote, "CornBread loves Cynthia" over and over, and they dated for a short time until she moved away. In an interview with a newspaper decades later, McCray admitted that he kept writing graffiti after that because he enjoyed the notoriety (being famous for something negative—in this case, an illegal activity) it gave him. He said, "I was the only graffiti artist in the city of Philadelphia. For that matter, I was the only one in the world. The more people talked about CornBread, the more I wrote it. I wrote my name all over South Philly [and eventually] people were really sick and tired of seeing my name."[15]

Other tags soon began showing up, such as Cool Earl, Dr. Cool 1, Bobby Kidd, Sir Smooth, and Sherlock Holms. Cool Earl, who sometimes teamed up with CornBread to write graffiti, had a simple reason for what he did. "I started writing," he said, "to prove to people where I was. You go somewhere and get your name up there and people know you were there, that you weren't afraid."[16]

Graffiti artists made their tags famous by putting them in unusual spots. Bobby Kidd became legendary in Philadelphia for tagging a police car while a friend distracted its occupants. CornBread became Philadelphia's most daring graffiti artist by tagging an elephant at the zoo and the Jackson 5's private jet when the popular singing group went to Philadelphia to perform. McCray pulled off the plane stunt by hiding among Jackson 5 fans at Philadelphia International Airport. Amid the chaos fans caused when the group got off the plane, McCray sneaked away from the crowd and tagged the plane. Even though such acts are considered vandalism, McCray never felt he was doing anything terrible. "People [in gangs] got reputations for murdering people, stabbing people," McCray said. "I wanted a reputation as well, but I didn't want to hurt anybody for it."[17]

A few years after CornBread became famous in Philadelphia, similar graffiti began appearing in New York City, and graffiti flourished there as it had never done before.

Two Famous Tags

New Yorkers in the late 1960s began seeing "JULIO 204" scrawled on buildings and in the underground subway system. Julio combined his nickname with the street he lived on—204th Street—to create one of the most famous early New York tags.

Julio, though, never became as famous as TAKI 183, the graffiti artist whom historians claim was most responsible for igniting New York's modern graffiti craze.

In the summer of 1970, the 16-year-old high school student began writing on ice cream trucks near his

The Unwritten Rules

The graffiti community is considered by social sciences experts to be a subculture—"a culture within a broader mainstream culture, with its own separate values, practices, and beliefs."[1] For instance, in mainstream culture, it is considered important to report illegal activity to the police. However, in the graffiti subculture, most of their activities are illegal, and reporting a fellow graffiti artist to the police would give the artist who went to the police a bad reputation. There are other unwritten rules of the graffiti subculture; not everyone follows them and some may be different in different places, but in general, they include:

- Writing over another artist's work will provoke a fight.
- Beginners cannot write over experts' work.
- The way to gain fame within the community is by impressing a more experienced artist.
- If it is legal, it is not graffiti.
- Religious structures and small businesses are off-limits.

1. "Subculture," Chegg Study. www.chegg.com/homework-help/definitions/subculture-49.

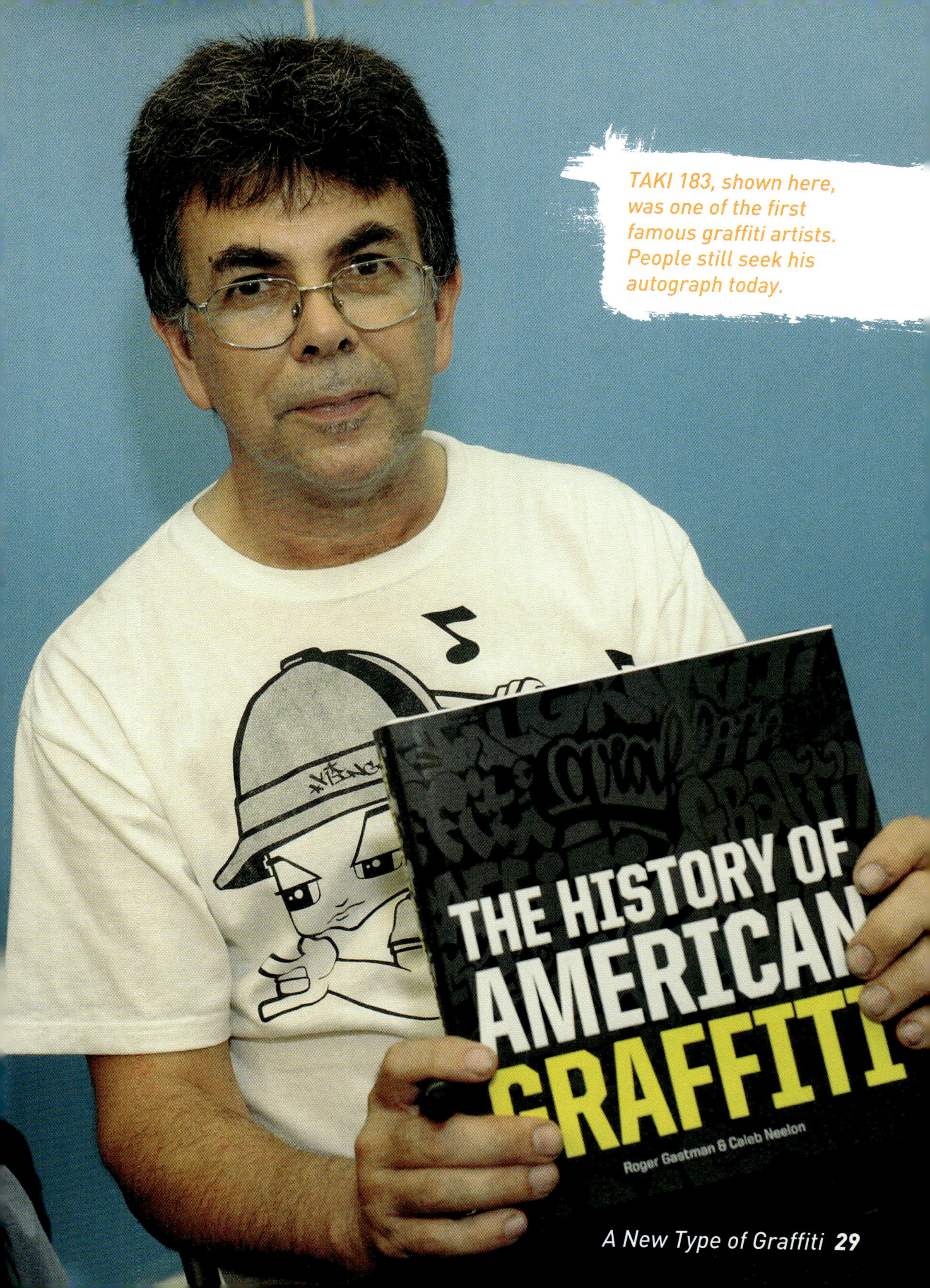

TAKI 183, shown here, was one of the first famous graffiti artists. People still seek his autograph today.

home. His tag was composed of a nickname for his Greek first name, Demetrius, and the street he lived on in his Washington Heights neighborhood. Unlike previous graffiti artists who never strayed from their neighborhoods, TAKI wrote his tag throughout the city. A job he had later as a messenger delivering packages helped him place his tag in so many different places in the giant city that the *New York Times* ran a story in 1971 about why he was doing it. TAKI told a reporter who tracked him down that he began doing graffiti because he was bored. He said, "I didn't have a job then and you pass the time, you know. I took the form from JULIO 204, but he was doing it for a couple of years then and he was busted and stopped. I just did it everywhere I went. I still do, though not as much. You don't do it for girls; they don't seem to care. You do it for yourself."[18]

In 2009, Roger Gastman, one of the authors of the book *The History of American Graffiti*, contacted TAKI and convinced him to write a foreword to the book and sell some of his work online. The *New York Times* interviewed him again in 2011, and he gave his thoughts about the evolution of modern graffiti: "I think a lot of what the graffiti movement spawned, early on, was just vandalism and defacement. But later on real artists started doing it, and it did become a true art form."[19]

Giving Young People an Outlet

Graffiti historian Cedar Lewisohn believes the development of modern graffiti starting in the 1960s marked an important advancement in art. He wrote,

> *In cultural terms, the [graffiti explosion] was a unique phenomenon. Its importance cannot be over-estimated. The phenomenon of dispossessed young people in New York City in the 1970s [who were] channeling their frustrations and boredom into making visual art—not music, not sport but art—is unprecedented. The art form they invented helped them to start to view the world in terms of all the visual languages that were available to them as sources to quote from and remix. We see this in piece after piece that happily steals from elements of pop culture. All of this activity happened completely spontaneously, with no initial financial backing or incentive, and the first group of graffiti writers had little or no art-school training or knowledge. This was a remarkable achievement, and it could be argued, the most culturally significant art movement of the second half of the twentieth century. No other movement since Cubism or Surrealism has developed such a distinctly new language.*[1]

1. Cedar Lewisohn, *Street Art: The Graffiti Revolution*. New York, NY: Abrams, 2008, p. 31.

The Graffiti Movement Grows

Graffiti continued to grow in other major cities during the 1970s, but New York was where the most admired graffiti came from. Nicholas Ganz has written several books on modern graffiti. In *Graffiti World: Street Art from Five Continents*, Ganz explained why graffiti blossomed so strongly in New York:

> *The unique make-up of New York City—in which the Harlem slums and the glamorous world of Broadway stand side by side—seems to have been a breeding-ground for the first graffiti artists, bringing together many different cultures and classes in one single place. This environment fueled an artistic battle against the power brokers in society, and a breakaway from poverty and the ghetto.*[20]

Most graffiti artists came from inner-city neighborhoods plagued by social problems, such as poverty, a lack of education, and crime. Most artists were also Latinx or black, marking a strong contrast to the past when most well-known artists had been white, wealthy, and educated. Mico, who is of Puerto Rican descent, was one of the early graffiti artists. Mico said he and other artists were motivated by a simple goal. He explained, "It began in different neighborhoods. But we all had one thing in common: We wanted to be famous ... [It] was just about getting up [a tag], getting around. The more hits [tags] you had, the more famous you became."[21]

Such fame was especially important to young people from impoverished backgrounds. Herbert Kohl was a New York teacher who tutored Johnny Rodriguez, a 13-year-old Puerto Rican boy who had dropped out of school because he could barely read and write. Kohl became intrigued with graffiti when he noticed that Rodriguez was scribbling "Bolita" on the elevator doors and halls of Kohl's apartment building before and after lessons. Kohl learned that Bolita—Spanish for "little ball"—was the nickname Rodriguez's mother had given him. Rodriguez stopped writing in Kohl's building when Kohl asked him to. However, when Kohl began seeing "Bolita as Johnny Cool" and other similar tags near his apartment building, he knew Rodriguez had written them. Kohl noticed that when he saw Rodriguez on the street, he seemed to be more confident and outgoing than he was during lessons. Kohl attributed that to the psychological boost Rodriguez got from seeing his tag in public. He explained, "Johnny appeared in a different perspective to me [on the street] because of the way he was described on the wall. [He] seemed like another person on the streets—or perhaps it would be more appropriate to say that he was another person with me during lessons."[22]

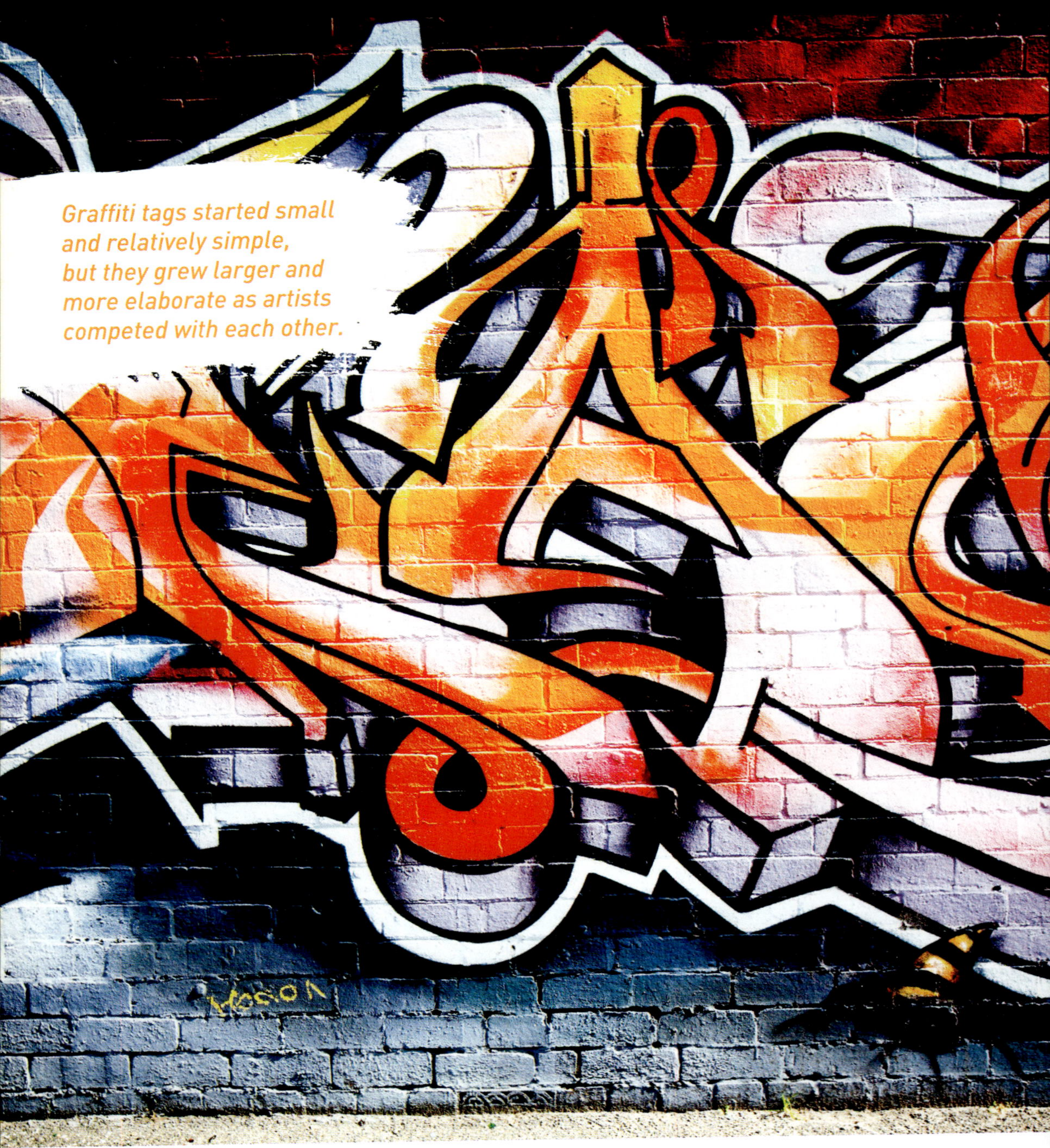

Graffiti tags started small and relatively simple, but they grew larger and more elaborate as artists competed with each other.

The ego boost Rodriguez got from becoming known for his tag is a major reason so many people write graffiti. That same psychological need for recognition among their peers also led graffiti artists to quit writing their names in simple letters. In their attempts to be the best, they began creating bigger and more elaborate tags, and their work eventually became a visual art phenomenon.

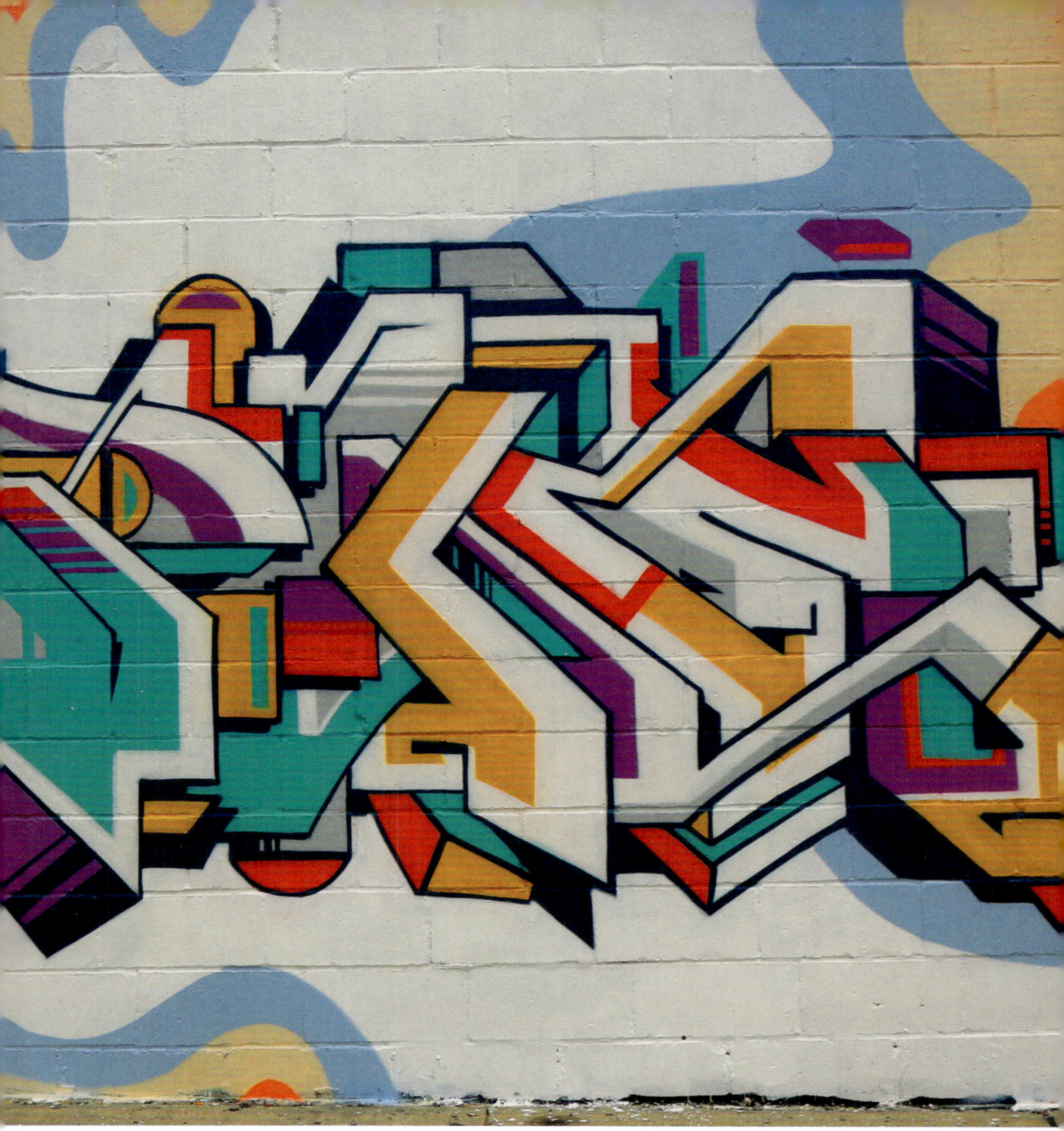

A Changing Art Form

The earliest graffiti tags were done in marker, were fairly small, and had simple lettering. Mico said competition among artists changed that. He explained, "The letters got more refined and larger and larger. We were each trying to outdo the other."[23] The easiest way to make tags more dramatic was to use spray paint instead of markers.

Graffiti also became more elaborate as writers—the term generally used for

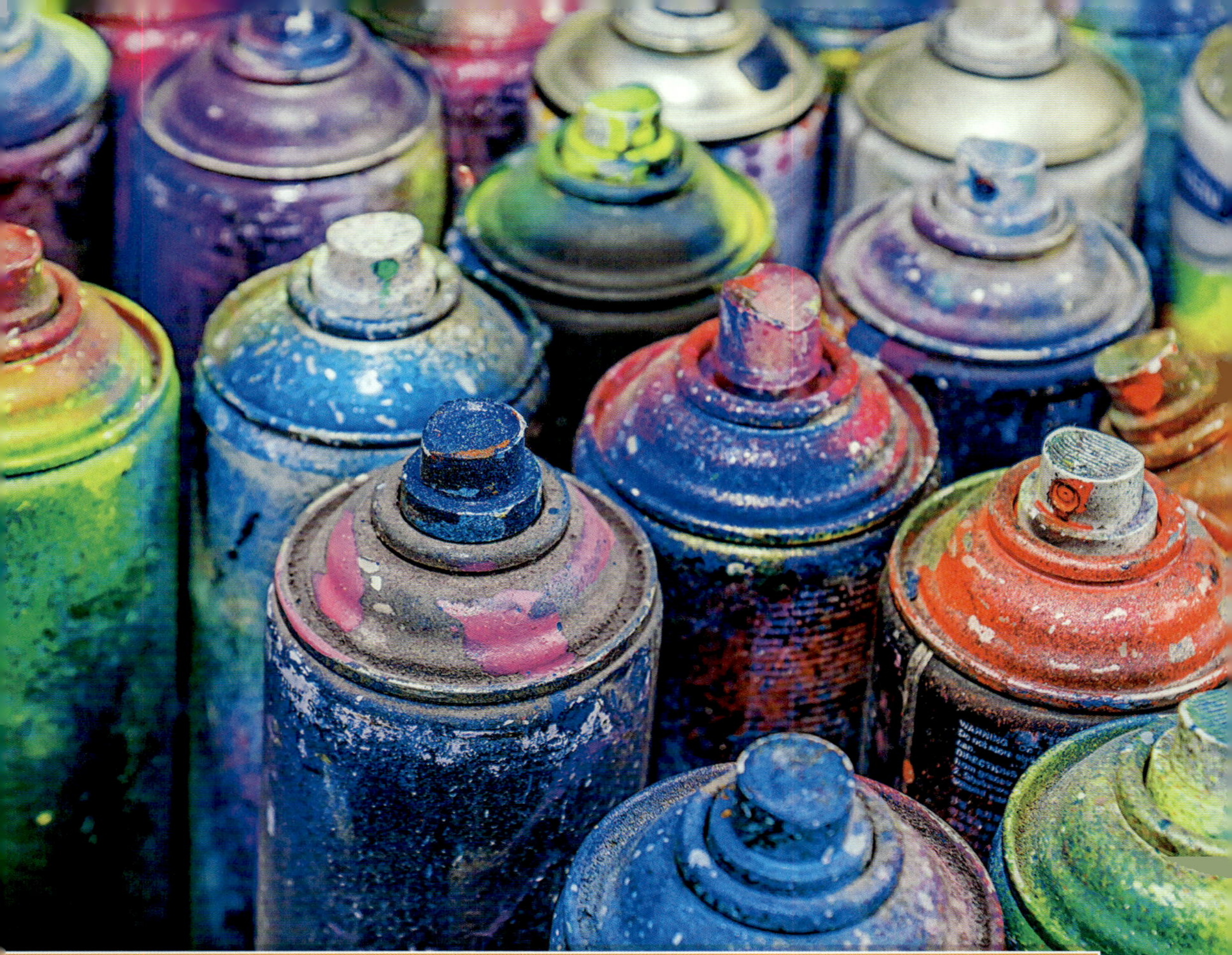

Spray paint and markers have always been the most popular materials for modern graffiti artists.

people who simply tag their name rather than creating drawings—began using creative letter styles to make their tags more interesting.

A style called Broadway elegant has long, thin, closely packed letters. Bubble style features fat letters that are often oddly shaped and outlined with a different color. Graffiti artist Phase 2, whose real name is Lonny Wood, is widely credited with the invention of bubble style. Geographers David Ley and Roman Cybriwsky said the highly styled lettering makes the tags mini works of art. They explained, "The signature is distinctive. It is usually spray-painted from an aerosol can and is highly accentuated, embellished with elegant curves and generous serifs. The letters, like the name itself, convey a message of 'style.'"[24]

Graffiti experts generally agree that wildstyle is the hardest to master. It is complex, combining interlocking and overlapping letters with decorations such as dots and arrows. People who

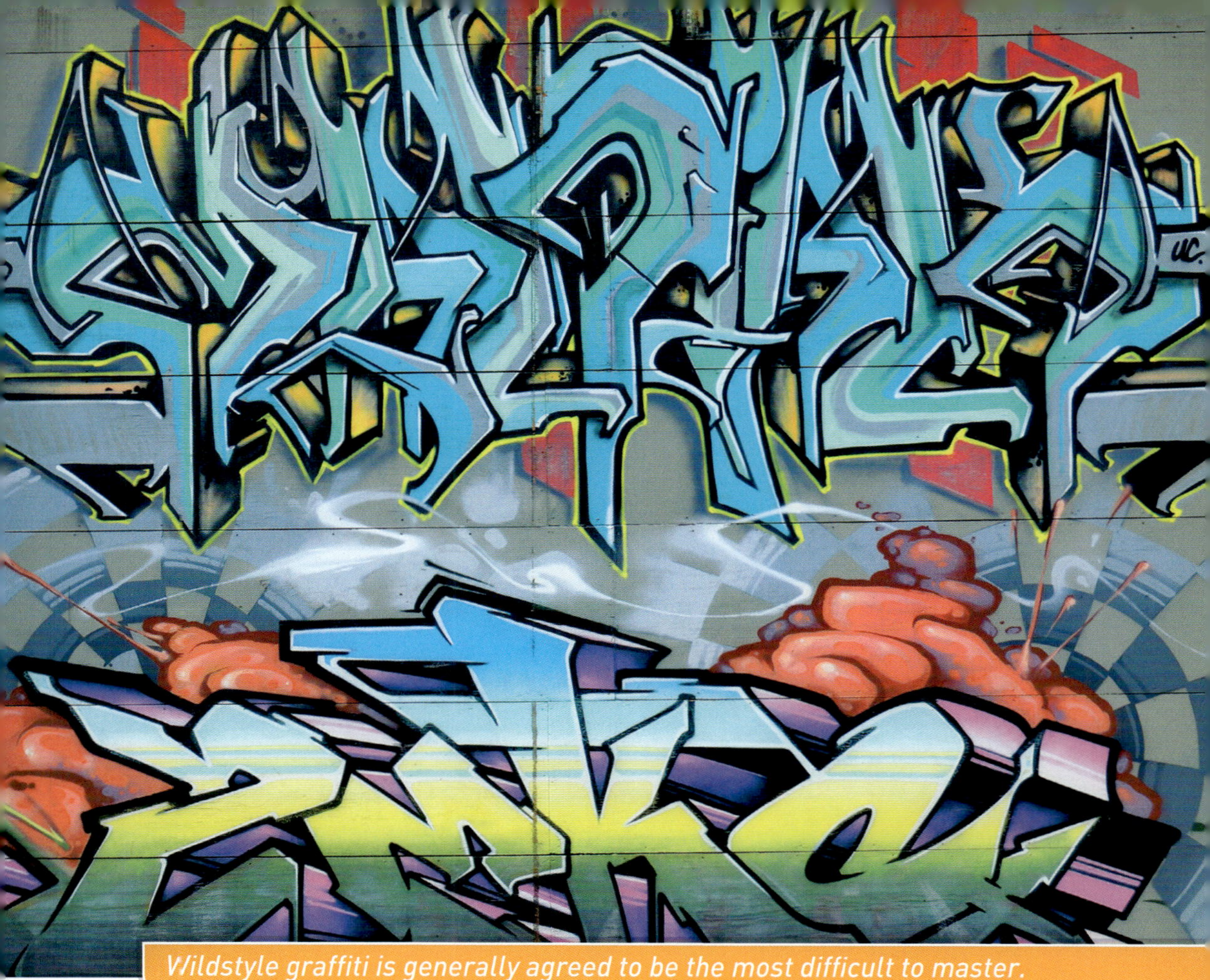

Wildstyle graffiti is generally agreed to be the most difficult to master.

are unfamiliar with graffiti often cannot read wildstyle, "but each graffiti artist actually follows a set pattern and technique, which means that wildstyle graffiti can be interpreted by those in the know, or people with the patience to decode a wildstyle piece."[25] People who are familiar with a certain artist's style may become able to identify pieces by that artist based on the details they include in a work.

Graffiti styles evolved rapidly in just a few years, even though the artists had to invent them as they were doing it. Eric Haze, who began doing graffiti in 1972 and today is a graphic designer, described its early development: "There was still no blueprint [so artists with] a few cans of paint combined with their desire for self expression created what [is] perhaps the only other truly American art form born [in the 20th century] in the wake of jazz."[26]

The ultimate goal of artists who pioneered modern graffiti was to be noticed—and they achieved that quickly by the sheer volume of what they wrote.

A Common Sight

There were two ways early graffiti artists earned recognition from their peers as "kings," or masters of the art: by putting up a huge number of tags or by placing them in hard-to-get spots. If a prolific writer writes hundreds of tags in one area, it is called "killing" or "bombing."

Some artists enjoy the challenge of targets that are hard to hit because they are in places that are always crowded or where security is tight. Others do it because it is one of the quickest ways to achieve fame. A female graffiti artist who called herself STONEY struggled to gain respect in the male-dominated field and only succeeded when she tagged the Statue of Liberty in 1972.

Typically, graffiti artists try to do things that will impress other graffiti artists rather than the general public. They know that while many people will not understand the difficulty of some of their feats, other artists will. Graffiti artist Cameron Moberg said,

> *When people are looking for a spot, they want to choose one that other*

"A Cry for Change"

The Faith of Graffiti, published in 1974, was the first book that treated modern graffiti seriously as art. The book features hundreds of pictures of graffiti by photographers Jon Naar and Mervyn Kurlansky with several pages of text by famed novelist Norman Mailer. Naar, in a book he authored himself years later, claimed that people could not understand 1970s graffiti without knowing where the artists lived. He wrote:

> *As you read the street numbers on the tags and in photographs [you] will see that the vast majority of the writers came from the most-run-down and neglected sections of New York: Harlem, Washington Heights, the Bronx, and the Lower East Side. The writers, like the other inhabitants of those districts at that time, were predominantly Hispanic and African-American. The graffiti they sprayed on the fronts of homes [and] on the trains that ran through their neighborhoods were a cry for change from the ghetto to clean up the filthy streets, to improve the quality of the schools, and to reduce the glaring inequities between rich and poor. Via the trains and buses the writers sent their message to more affluent parts of the city as well as leaving their marks on (mostly) public spaces.*[1]

1. Jon Naar, *The Birth of Graffiti*. New York, NY: Prestel, 2007, p. 19.

graffiti writers will see and say, 'Dang, how did he get that spot?' ... That can be crazy in a couple of ways—it can just be really high or it can be in a spot that's really public and it's like, 'How'd he do that with so many people around?'[27]

By the early 1970s, so many people were tagging every available blank public space that it began to be difficult to find room to write more tags. One of the most popular places to tag had been the inside of subway cars but, as space filled up, people began writing on the outside of the cars. In the 1970s, New York's subway cars became the backdrop for some of the wildest, most brazen, and most artistic graffiti ever produced.

CHAPTER THREE

The Evolution of Graffiti

Graffiti is a constantly evolving art form. Graffiti writers and street artists develop their own individual styles, which often influence others in the graffiti community, creating even more new styles. It is a unique art form because works often must be completed quickly so the artist can avoid being caught and arrested, and most graffiti is temporary—it is often either removed by public officials or painted over by other artists. These two factors influence the way graffiti artists create their works.

Art historians consider the mid-1970s to the late 1980s to be the golden age of graffiti. One of the leading graffiti artists of the time was Leonard Hilton McGurr in New York, whose tag was Futura 2000, which he changed to just Futura after the year 2000. During this period, McGurr saw graffiti transformed from simple tags done in marker to complex works of spray paint art. McGurr said, "If you look at graffiti in New York in the early 70s, it was whack [not cool], it was very crude. I'm speaking unholy words—because we're talking about the Mecca [of graffiti]—but it took us time to work out what we were doing, since we were inventing as we went along."[28]

McGurr's abstract and artistic designs influenced the more complex lettering that helped graffiti grow and change from stylized writing into a full-fledged art form. A major factor in this evolution was that graffiti artists began working

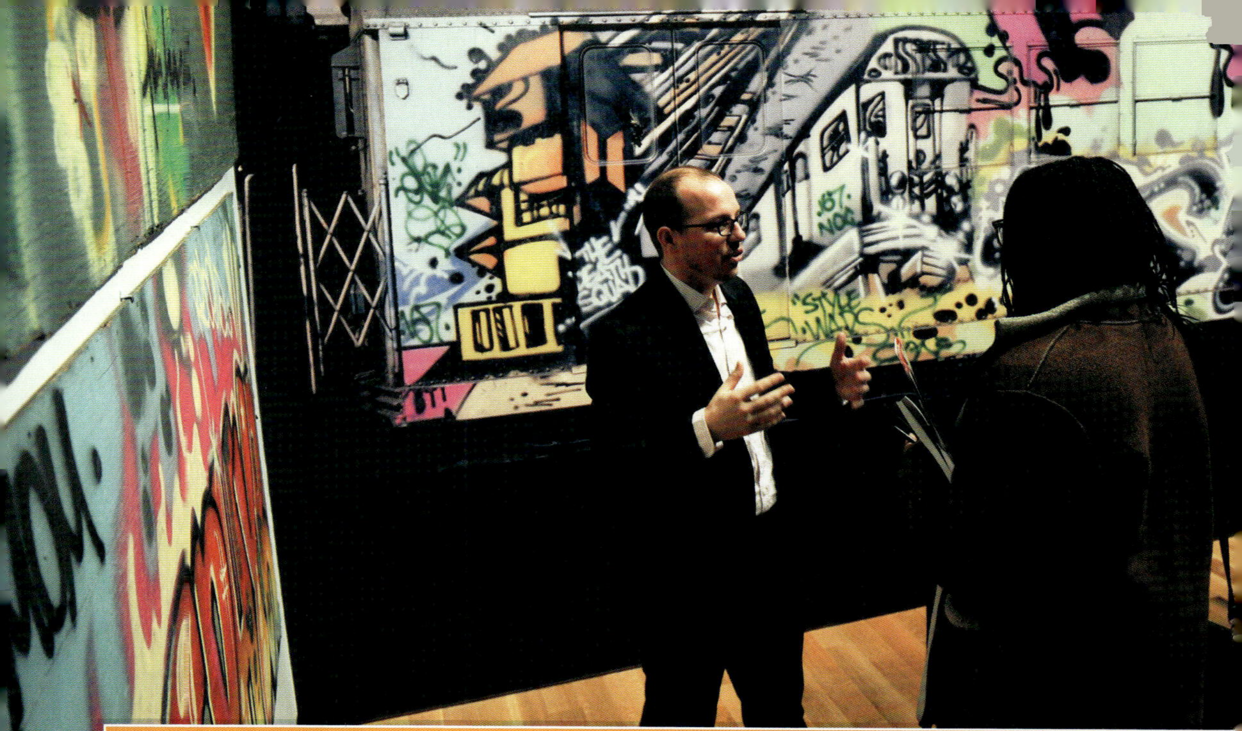

In the 1970s and 1980s, many New Yorkers did not like their subway cars covered with graffiti. Today, however, the old cars are considered historical works of art and are sometimes shown in museums.

on much bigger spaces, which allowed them to let their imaginations and their creativity expand onto the huge surfaces they covered. Although some artists still used blank walls and other public spaces, the most daring and creative made the exteriors of subway cars their canvas of choice. They did this because they knew the cars would make their tags famous by allowing millions of people to see their work as they moved through the giant city.

New York City subway cars are 75 feet (23 m) long and 12 feet (3.7 m) high. Tags consisting of brightly colored, twisting letters and whimsical figures often ran the length of a car, and a few were several cars long. The speed with which the cars flashed by people in subway stations made the mobile art works look amazing even when the cars were not standing still. Claes Oldenburg, one of the 20th century's most honored sculptors, loved the spray-painted cars. Oldenburg believed the cars added a needed touch of color to the city. He said, "You're standing there in the station, everything is gray and gloomy and all of a sudden one of those graffiti trains slides in and brightens the place like a big bouquet [of flowers]."[29]

Like other graffiti, what became known as subway art is illegal. However, the possibility of being arrested by police or security guards added to the respect, or "cred" (short for "credibility"), artists earned from each other.

A Risky Activity

To paint New York subway cars, artists had to climb or cut fences to enter holding yards and layups, the aboveground areas where extra cars are stored on weekends and during non-rush hours when there are not as many riders. These areas are at the ends of the lines in areas such as the Bronx, Queens, and Brooklyn. The work was generally done at night, which meant the artists, most of whom were teenagers, had to sneak away from home and brave the dangers of New York's crime-ridden city streets to find a car to paint.

Lee Quiñones, who was born in Puerto Rico and grew up in New York, began painting subway cars in 1974 when he was 14 years old. Before he stopped writing graffiti a decade later to create paintings and other more traditional art, Quiñones had made his tag,

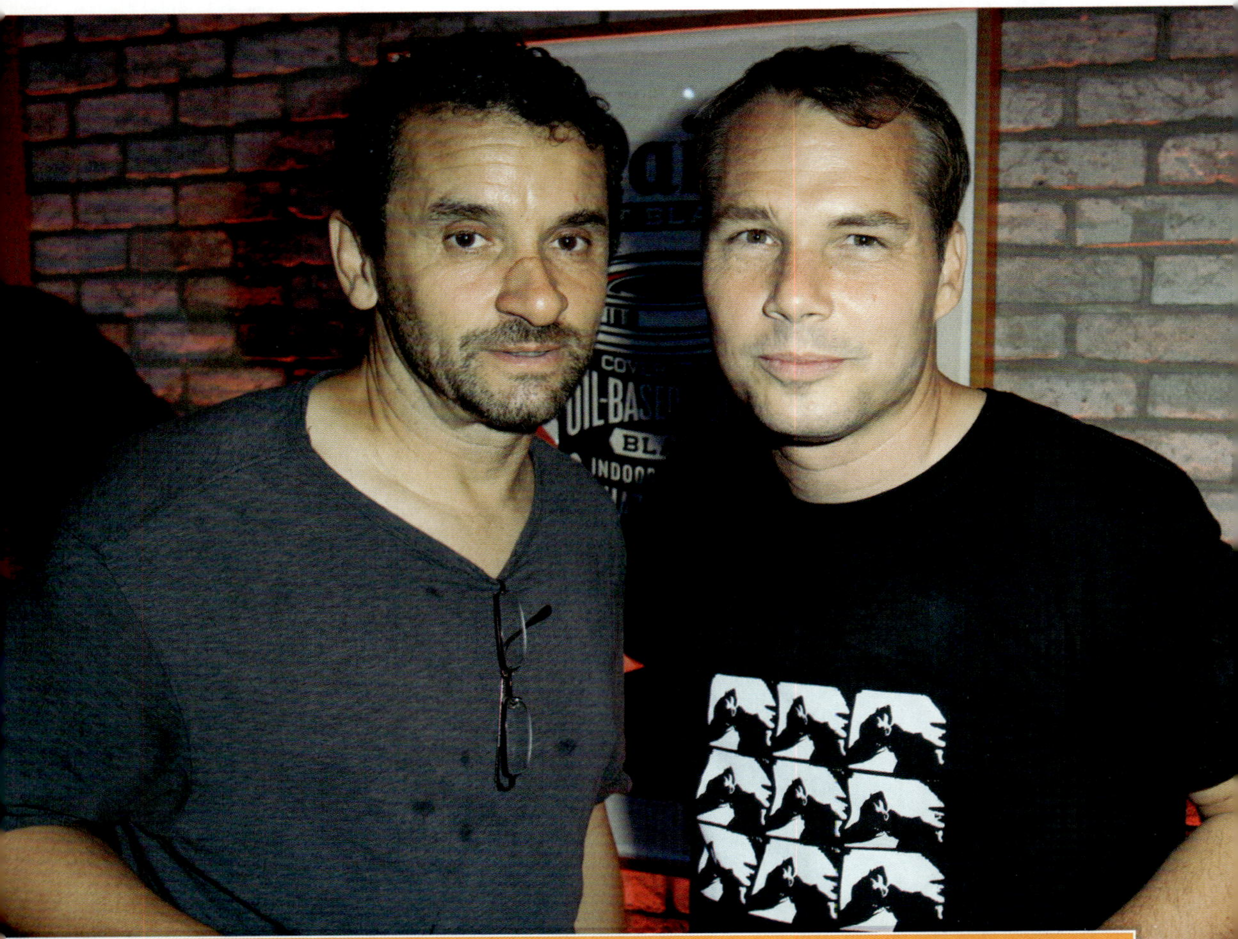

Some graffiti artists, such as Lee Quiñones (left), end up making and selling their art legally.

"Lee," one of the era's most famous. Among his accomplishments was painting an estimated 115 whole subway cars. In November 1976, he and five other artists known as the Fabulous Five managed the seemingly impossible feat of covering all ten cars in one train from top to bottom with colorful graffiti—the only time one group painted an entire train. Quiñones is proud of the art he created, but years later, he admitted it had been dangerous. He recalled, "My mother feared for my life, 'cause I was leaving home in the middle of the night and coming back in the early morning, when I was supposed to be going to school that day—but I wasn't … [At] any given time, I could've met death."[30]

Some graffiti writers did come to harm. In the book *The Faith of Graffiti*, author Norman Mailer noted that one young man was killed beneath a subway car while painting it and another was seriously burned when a paint can caught fire from a spark.

One danger was that the subway cars sat on three rails, including one with live current to propel them when needed. Mico said the teen writers ignored such dangers to paint graffiti. He explained, "When you're young, you don't really realize the danger you're putting your behind in. You don't realize that you're dealing with 600 volts of electricity [and that] people have gotten killed."[31] However, artist Japan 1 admitted, "I was scared all the time I did it."[32]

Artists often had to run from police officers and transit authority guards who would arrest or even hurt them. For instance, on September 28, 1983, 25-year-old Michael Stewart died after transit authority guards beat him for spray painting graffiti in a Manhattan subway station. However, writers kept coming back despite the dangers, and according to graffiti artist Stag 161, they were generally free to do their painting:

> *We would write out in the open. Citizens were intimidated to the point where they would not say anything. We had free reign over the yards and lay-ups. Yes, there were token arrests, but while one guy was being escorted out the south side of the tunnel, there would be three or four more writers on the north side still carrying on with their craft.*[33]

For many, the risks seemed well worth it. Sandra Fabara, who made the tag "Lady Pink" famous, was one of the first female graffiti artists. Fabara, who grew up in New York but was born in Ecuador, began painting cars when she was 15 years old. "I was already famous as soon as I started, just because I was a girl,"[34] Fabara said. "I was attracted to the adventure, the rebelliousness of it. The more guys said, 'You can't do it,' the more I wanted to do it. It was the risk of it, but also having fun, to be cool and popular."[35] Fabara showed males she was worthy of joining them by ignoring danger and working hard to become a good artist.

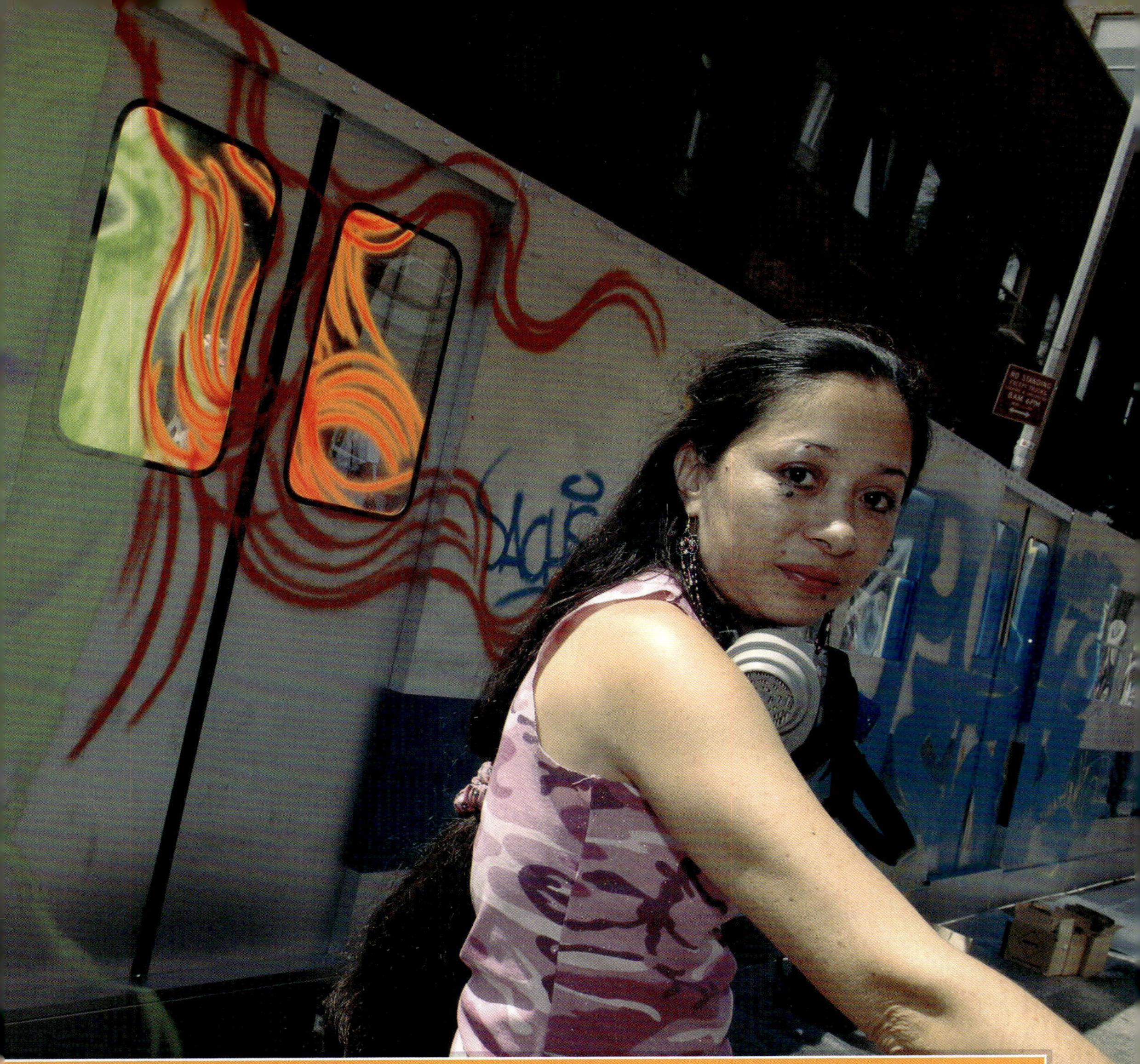

Sandra Fabara, shown here, better known as Lady Pink, helped prove that female graffiti artists could be just as good as male artists.

In contrast to most arts, part of the skill of graffiti writing is the ability artists need to avoid the dangers involved in doing their art. In the 1980s, Alain Maridueña tagged subway cars as KET. Maridueña continued creating graffiti and studying it around the world even after the subway era ended. In 2009, he stated, "Train writing was and is a movement that involved skill, stealth and heart."[36] The artists needed to develop skills, such as locating a subway car to paint and evading authorities long enough to finish their work, just to do the art they loved.

Can Control

Spray paint has always been the most popular material for graffiti artists, which means they must become experts at using it effectively—a process they call "can control." Graffiti artist Cameron Moberg explained,

Can control is essentially being able to use the can properly and being able to manipulate what the can does ... For example, when you have something called a flare it's when it's really wide and fuzzy at the top of a letter and as you get to the bottom it will be really clean and skinnier. That can control process is not just moving your arm, it's moving your wrist, rotating your wrist and arm at the same time. In the '90s, we didn't have the paint we have now. We were using hardware store paint which is really runny and it takes a lot of commitment to learn how to use.[1]

1. Quoted in Kelly Bryant, "12 Things You Probably Didn't Know about Street Art," Mental Floss, February 3, 2015. mentalfloss.com/article/61441/12-things-you-probably-didnt-know-about-street-art.

Becoming More Detailed

When graffiti's golden era began in the 1970s, artists simply wrote their names on subway cars in larger letters than they had used inside the same cars. However, because they had more time in the deserted storage areas, they were able to create complex, unique tags that took up so much space they began calling them "pieces," a term that, in the graffiti world, is short for "masterpiece." Artists also invented new terms for other, even grander works—a "panel piece" was graffiti painted between the doors and below the windows of a subway car, while "blockbuster" was a wide-lettered graffiti style that stretched the length of a car. Steven Ogburn, one of the writers who is credited with inventing the latter style, explained why he began writing his tag, "Blade," so big: "I wanted to make sure you could see a train from five blocks away and you could read it. COMET 1 and myself invented the blockbuster [style] in 1980: very large, square words, but very legible. We painted over 5,000 trains each, over the span of those years."[37]

Even though aerosol cans enabled people to write tags more quickly, it took subway artists a long time to cover an entire car. Super-Kool 223, who is credited by some historians with having created the first graffiti piece, discovered that spray nozzles from consumer products such as oven cleaner could be transplanted onto paint cans to produce a wider spray. The innovation was called a "fat cap," and it helped artists do their work even more quickly.

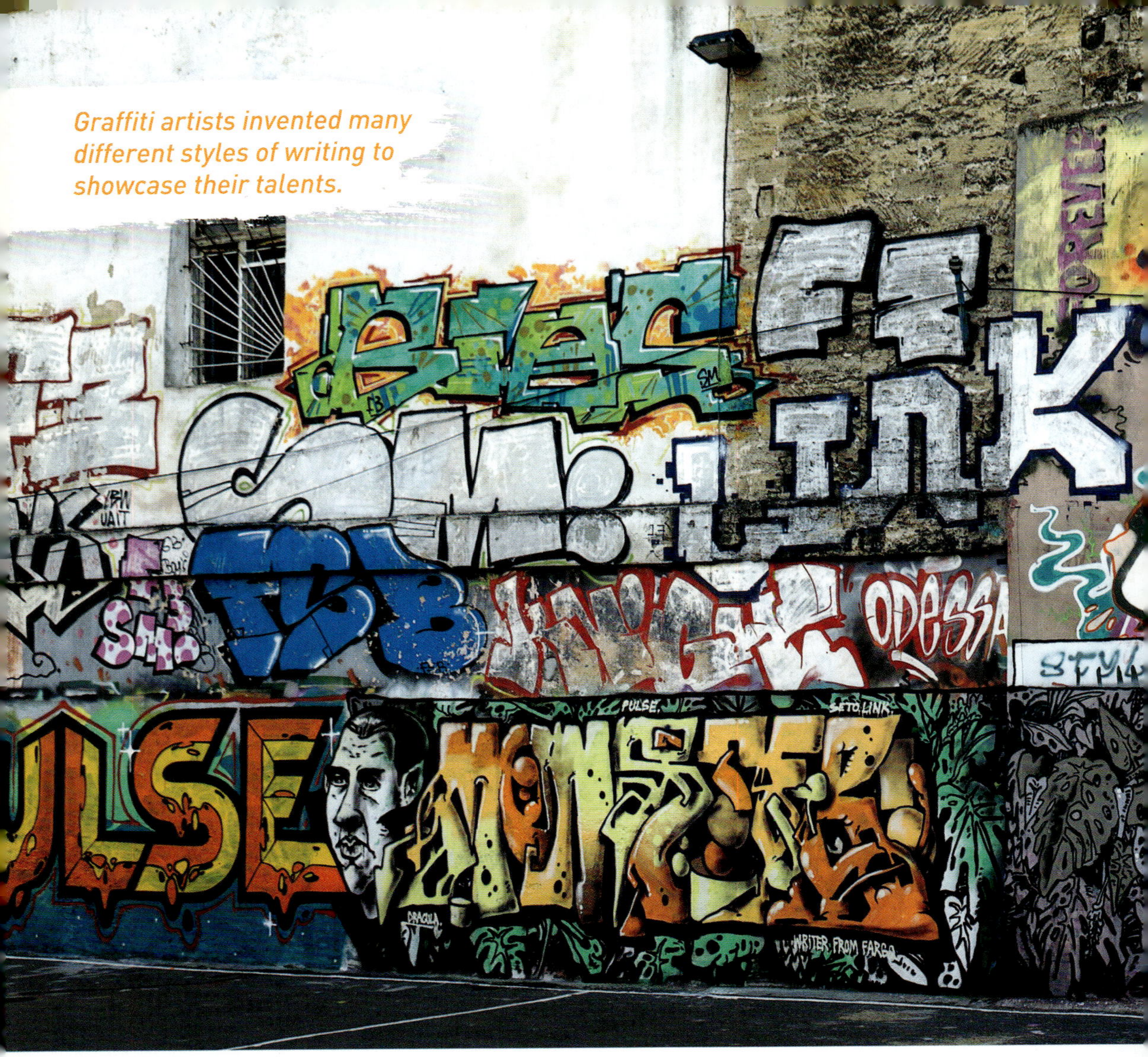

Graffiti artists invented many different styles of writing to showcase their talents.

However, using a fat cap, or any spray can for that matter, is not easy. Graffiti historian Jack Stewart explained how difficult it is to learn spray-can technique: "It is extremely hard to keep spray paint from dripping when spraying on a vertical surface, and even respected artists occasionally had trouble with it. From the beginning, dripping paint was the most obvious mark of a toy."[38]

Learning to control the spray was only a small part of the education of a "toy," the term for a beginner or someone who was not very good. Serious graffiti artists had many other techniques to master, such as how to overlap letters creatively while still leaving them readable and how to give letters a three-dimensional effect through the use of complex shading.

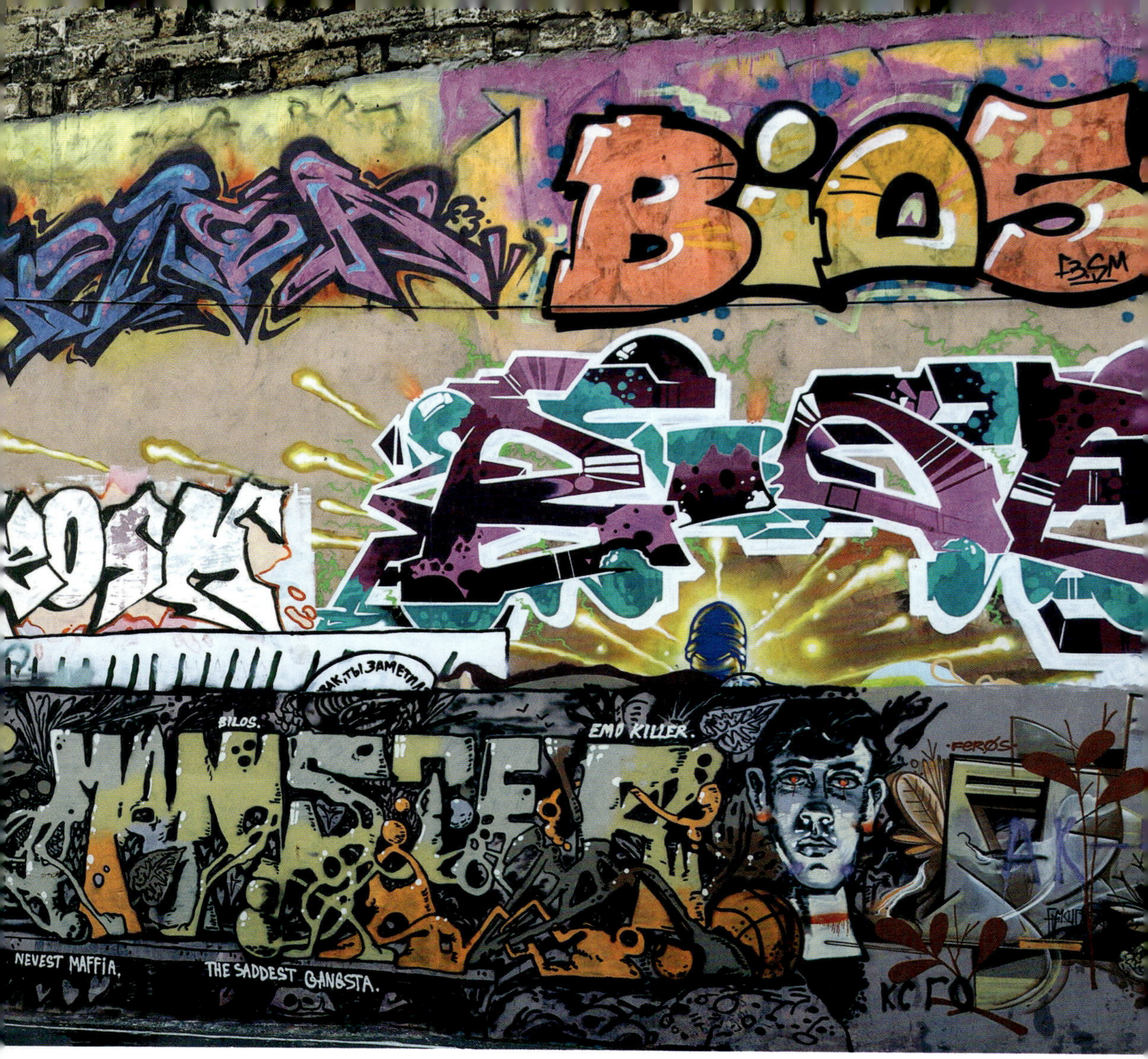

In addition to fat caps, artists used other caps that produced fine sprays so they could outline their work or create details such as arrows and hearts. Artists also began adding abstract shapes and caricatures of people and animals to their tags. They even borrowed characters from popular culture, such as video game characters. In 1983, writers Son 1 and Rem painted a Mario Brothers–like figure on a train in Manhattan, New York.

Full-car creations were the most impressive. In 1980, Ogburn drew his tag name across a subway car in black, fat, squiggly letters against a pink and red background. The tag looked menacing and its letters, outlined and shaded in white and gray, appeared three-dimensional. That same year, Donald J. White, one of the most famous and most respected subway writers, covered a car from top to bottom with fat, tilted letters spelling out his tag, "Dondi." According to the art website Widewalls, "Although Dondi was capable of producing the classic wildstyle form of graffiti writing, he preferred and developed his original large block style, which has remained influential to this day, allowing people to be able to read the text and also [enabling] Dondi to create patterns within the letters."[39] Works of all sizes and in every shade imaginable decorated the cars, and most had stylistic quirks that gave them a unique look. Some lettering was so stylized as to be nearly unreadable, but that did not take away from the exotic effect the colorfully painted cars created as they pulled into subway stations.

Most subway artists were dedicated to producing their creations and took great pride in them. Super-Kool was one of the artists who turned New York's subway system into a mobile art show. He and his fellow artists loved watching their subway art rush by them. In 1974, he said, "I sometimes go on Sunday to the Seventh Avenue and 6th Street station and just spend my whole day watching my name go by."[40] However, those feelings were bittersweet because many people who saw the graffiti considered it vandalism and not art. Quiñones said that his subway art "rolled in its own private subterranean stage [the subway], which consisted of one of the world's largest audiences, but who never even noticed its life."[41] Even sadder for Quiñones than having his art ignored was the fact that, like other subway artists, he never knew when his creations would be wiped away by public officials.

New York's War on Graffiti

The artists who transformed New York's subway system into a rapidly moving art exhibit knew their work might not survive even one week. In addition to public officials who would buff out or paint over their work, they also had to contend with other graffiti artists who might alter or deface their art. Tracy 168, a legendary artist of this period, was especially upset when officials wiped out work he did in 1976, the year the United States celebrated its 200th birthday. He said, "I wrote GOD BLESS AMERICA for the bicentennial. I did three pieces in red, white, and blue, and it was so beautiful that the MTA [Metropolitan Transportation Authority] immediately painted over it. They couldn't let anyone know that [graffiti artists] loved America."[42]

Due to the diligence of authorities, the work of graffiti artists often existed for only a short time. However, some subway art has survived in photographs. Martha Cooper and Henry Chalfant took pictures of graffiti for years and eventually published their pictures in 1984 in the book Subway Art, one of the period's most important historical records. Chalfant became friends with the artists, who would alert him to new pieces they wanted him to photograph. Chalfant would have to figure out where and when the car would run on the subway lines and then wait in the proper station to take its picture. Chalfant wrote, "I was always working against time since I could never be sure if a piece would remain intact for very long. Somebody might cross it out or the Transit [officials] could 'buff' it. I felt like I was stalking rare big game when I went out to take pictures of graffiti."[43]

As graffiti began to clutter buildings and subway cars, a large segment of the public became opposed to it. Many people did not appreciate the art. Others rejected it because it was vandalism of private property or were angry about the cost of cleaning it up. A 1972 *New York Times* opinion article stated, "The graffiti are no longer amusing; they have become a public menace."[44]

Many graffiti works are temporary; city officials and people who view graffiti as vandalism often wash it off or paint over it.

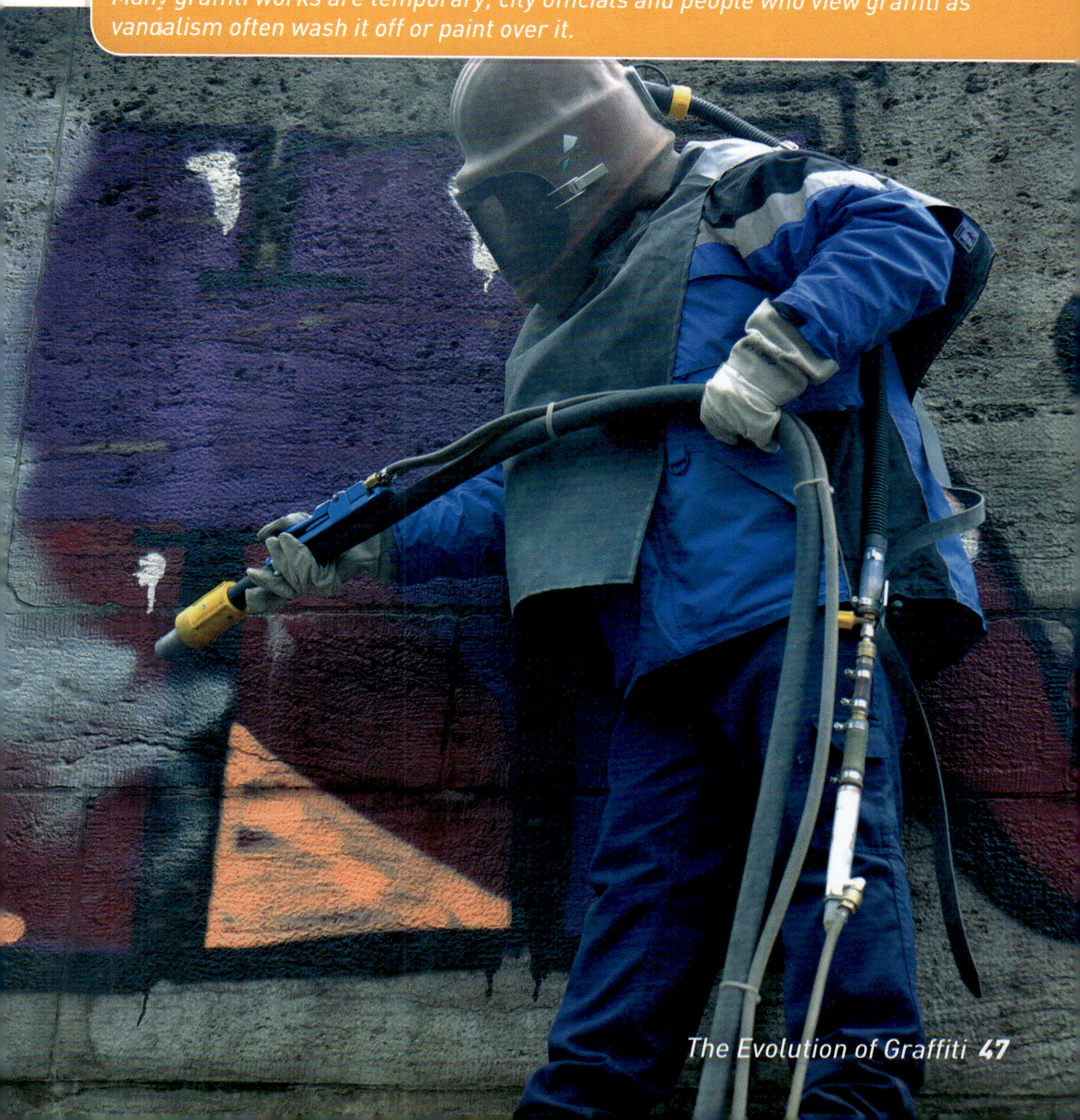

Graffiti Glossary

BITE: To copy another writer's style.

BLOCKBUSTER: A graffito with wide letters that extends from end to end on a subway car below the level of the car's window.

BOMB: The term for when a writer creates so many graffiti works that his or her work is noticed because of its quantity.

BUFF: The term for when graffiti is removed.

BURN: The term for when a writer or crew tags an area before fellow writers.

CAP: A nozzle on a spray paint can; it can be either fat or skinny depending on the size of the spray the cap produces.

CREW: A group of writers who band together to create graffiti.

CROSSING OUT: Adding something to another writer's work, crossing it out, or defacing it. Such acts show disrespect to the original artist.

GETTING UP: The term for when artists are noticed because they have so many signed graffiti.

HIT: A generic term for any graffiti piece.

KILL: What happens when one area is covered excessively with graffiti.

KING: A graffiti artist considered the best in the style he or she works in.

PIECE BOOK or **BLACK BOOK**: The book in which artists sketch their works and the works of other artists.

RACKING or **RACKING UP**: Another term for shoplifting; some writers steal their paint supplies, either because they cannot afford them or they are trying to establish cred.

TAG: As a noun, it refers to the name a graffiti artist signs on his work; as a verb, it means to create a piece of graffiti on any surface.

THROW-UP: A graffiti work that has to be done speedily so the artist is not caught doing it.

WRITER: Anyone who creates graffiti.

Starting in the early 1970s, city officials such as New York mayor John Lindsay began fighting to wipe out graffiti. In addition to a campaign to erase painted trains and increase subway security, New York passed a law banning the sale of spray paint to minors. The efforts failed to stem the rising tide of graffiti. The paint ban did not work because most artists preferred to steal their paint, and those who bought it often did so outside of New York City. New York was struggling so much financially in that period that it did not have enough money to arrest many of the artists.

According to Chalfant, the graffiti crackdown failed at first because it highlighted the art's illegal nature, which made it more fun and challenging for artists. Eventually, however, the cleanup crusade took its toll on artists. Chalfant wrote, "I would say by '83, '84, there were really good artists dropping out. They'd work and work, and their stuff wouldn't run [on subway lines] or it would get crossed out by some jerk."[45]

The end came in 1989, when New York City finally had enough money to increase subway security and keep artists out of storage areas. Security measures included patrolling the areas with dogs. The city also began taking painted cars out of service immediately, which dismayed some artists so much that they quit. Even though graffiti artists continued working on walls and other public spaces, the end of subway art also brought an end to what some consider to have been graffiti's greatest period of creativity.

Issues Within the Graffiti Community

Some people argue that the golden age of graffiti was not the end of graffiti's creativity, but the beginning. Modern-day street artists built off the foundations laid by the artists of the 1970s and 1980s, using their ideas in new, original ways. Changes in the materials artists use—for instance, spray paint that is less runny and easier to control—have allowed people to develop new painting styles.

These innovations have changed the way artists paint, but they have not changed some of the issues graffiti artists face within their community. One of these is the search for respect from other graffiti artists. From the beginning, graffiti has been about impressing others within the community rather than the general public. This sometimes leads to conflict between artists when they try to show their superiority by covering up someone else's work with their own. According to street artist Kristin Adamczyk, "Part of writing on the street is you could go back there tomorrow and it's covered up because somebody dissed you or you don't know where you are and you've written on somebody's wall that they've already called. There's politics and drama and silly things."[46] When the graffiti is done by gangs, this type of fighting can lead to physical violence; however, the majority of graffiti artists are not in gangs and do not settle their differences with guns or other weapons.

Another issue related to respect is the struggle female artists have to be

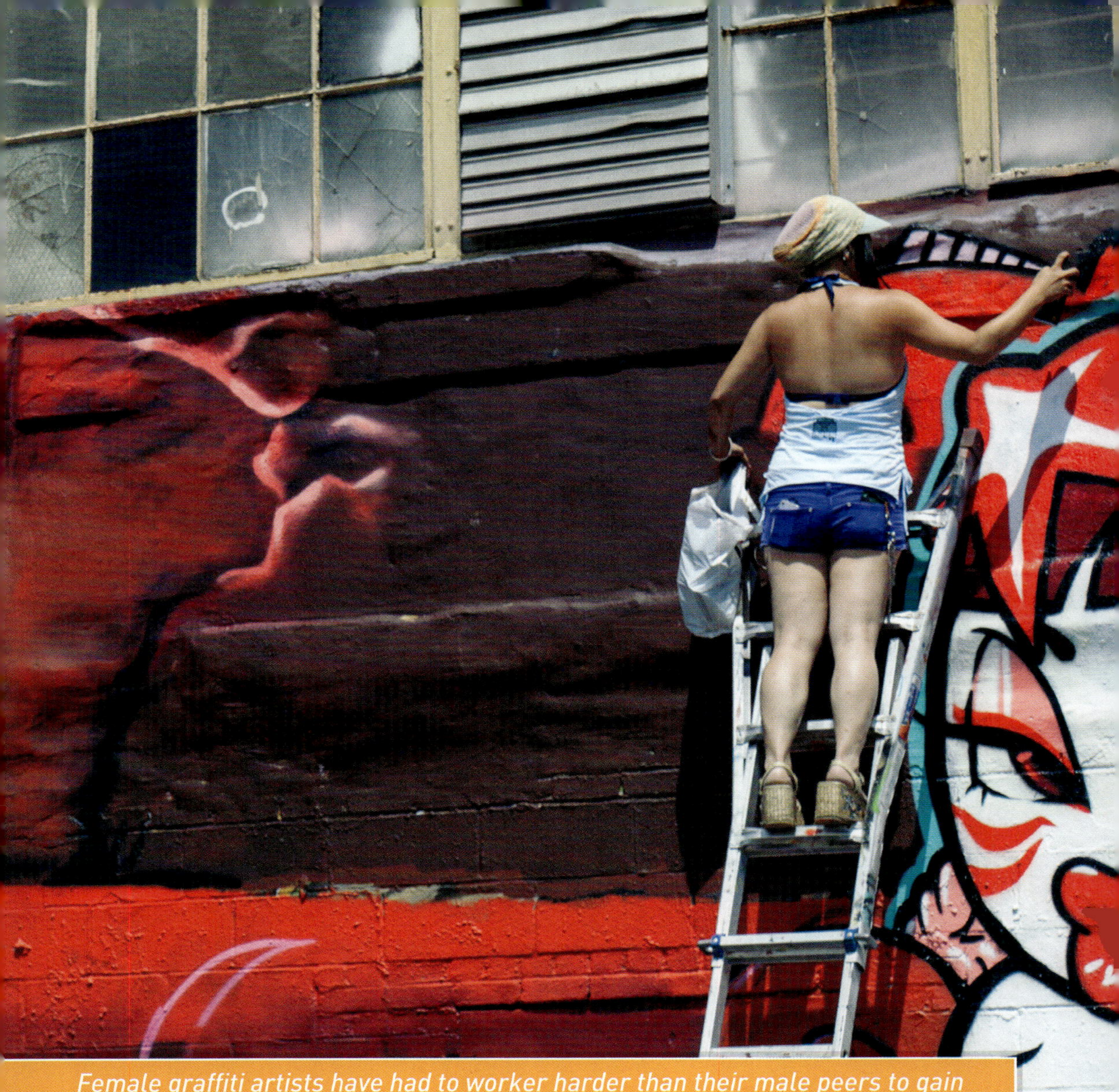

Female graffiti artists have had to worker harder than their male peers to gain acceptance of their work in the graffiti community.

accepted by their male peers. Social codes in the United States have always encouraged women to be quiet and stay out of trouble. As such, the illegal and dangerous nature of graffiti was considered by many male graffiti artists to make the activity unsuitable for women. This made it difficult for female artists to be taken seriously; many have described it as a "boys' club," where the men support each other and ignore the women. Female artist Cake described her experience in a group of male graffiti artists:

Graffiti Museums

Graffiti may have been considered ugly vandalism by many people in the 1980s, but by the early 21st century, attitudes had changed. Graffiti and street art are now considered by many to be works of art and are featured as exhibits in many museums. One reason for this attitude shift may be the change in style from simple tags to large, detailed, mural-like paintings; another may be that people who grew up seeing graffiti in many places view it as normal and even desirable because they are used to it.

In 2016, two museums dedicated specifically to graffiti and street art opened—the Graffiti and Street Art Museum of Texas in Houston and Art42 in Paris. Neither museum charges an admission fee, as people would not have to pay to see the art on the street. Art42 added to the original street experience by scattering the works around the museum. *Condé Nast Traveler* writer Lilit Marcus explained this unusual choice:

> *[Y]ou should be able to walk around a corner and be surprised by the art you stumble upon, just like you would out on the street ... If everything was behind a rope or labeled "please don't touch," the pieces would lose their outsider edge. Placing them among people helps keep the street art spirit alive, while also preserving the works and making sure they don't get torn down or painted over.*[1]

1. Lilit Marcus, "Art42 Is Paris's First Museum Dedicated to Street Art," *Condé Nast Traveler*, September 16, 2016. www.cntraveler.com/story/paris-is-getting-its-first-museum-dedicated-to-street-art.

> *It was sometimes difficult to feel equal when I first came on the scene. I often felt less than in a group of male graffiti or street artists. Like I was valued less, despite having a real and tangible talent that could back me up.*
>
> *There was one time a few of us were in a circle, a peer of ours just got picked up by the vandal squad, and they were all discussing it. I would chime in and when I did, I noticed no one would respond to me. I realized it was because they were hearing me, but they weren't acknowledging me. It was like I was a ghost, but really I think it was because I was female.*[47]

Many female graffiti artists also speak about the danger they face being out alone at night, especially in a big city. This is in addition to the danger graffiti artists face in the normal course of their work, such as climbing tall buildings and staying away from police.

Some male graffiti artists deny that graffiti is a boys' club; they say the important thing is not gender, but talent. Others acknowledge that while famous female graffiti artists are respected, it can be more difficult for a woman to gain that fame. Artist Scott Marsh said, "In graffiti … it's a lot harder to come up as a girl, there's a lot of … bravado in that scene. For that reason, there are not [a lot] of females in 'street art' with that 10 years plus graffiti background, which I think makes people strong artists."[48] Artist Dan Bergeron is hopeful that these negative attitudes toward female artists are changing over time: "I think it's probably the best time in the history of the world to be a female artist because there are more doors opening … Fifteen years ago, it would have been really tough for a woman to gain credibility and respect as part of the graffiti community."[49] However, many female artists believe that although things have improved over time, there is still a long way to go.

CHAPTER FOUR

Using Graffiti to Send a Message

Graffiti has often been used as a way for people to protest political and social aspects of society. From simple statements to elaborate paintings, people have found creative ways to make their disapproval known to the world. One of the best-known British graffiti artists goes by the name Banksy, and he became famous due to the messages his works sent, although no one knows his true identity. Most people assume Banksy is a man, but there is also speculation that the artist is a woman or even a group of people.

One of Banksy's famous works showed a young boy painting the words "One Nation Under CCTV" while a security guard photographed him. The work was a commentary on how little privacy people have in a high-tech world in which officials can use cameras to spy on people committing criminal offenses, such as writing graffiti. It created a sensation because Banksy had built a scaffolding three stories high to create it even though security cameras were monitoring his every action. Banksy believes artists have the right to create graffiti in public places to make political comments:

> *Bus stops are far more interesting and useful places to have art than in museums. Graffiti has more chance of meaning something or changing stuff than anything indoors. Graffiti has been used to start revolutions, stop wars, and generally is the voice*

of people who aren't listened to. [And] even if you don't come up with a picture to cure world poverty you can make somebody smile.[50]

Banksy may be one of the most well-known graffiti artists, but he is far from the only one using his work to send a message. Graffiti artists around the world use their works to comment on sexism and racism, criticize or support politicians and the decisions they make, and call people's attention to issues that are often overlooked in society.

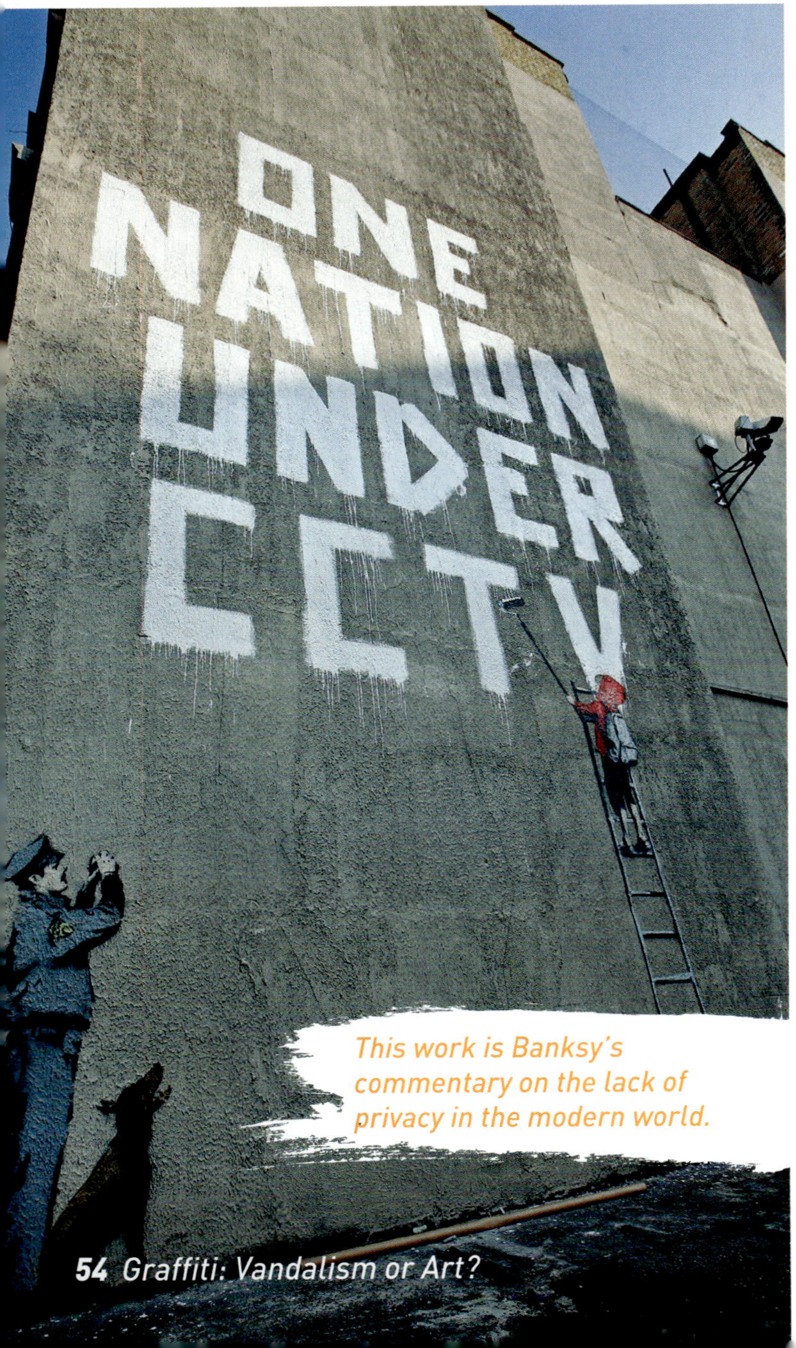

This work is Banksy's commentary on the lack of privacy in the modern world.

Making a Political Statement

Painting words on blank walls is a cheap and easy way to make a political statement. Authors Robert Reisner and Lorraine Wechsler believe that this is why the poorest and most humble people in any society have adopted this method through the ages to vent their anger and frustration or their support or opposition to various political issues. They also say that political graffiti can provide unique insights into the history of the periods in which they are written. Reisner and Wechsler wrote, "Graffiti are the voice of the common man. We are used to taking our history from aristocrats and statesmen and their paid scribes [public relations people]. But through graffiti we discovered evidence of another version of history, characterized by oppression and opposition to the official point of view."[51]

The oldest remains of political graffiti date back thousands of years. Graffiti historian Cedar Lewisohn wrote that graffiti in ancient Rome "was a popular way of speaking back to authority. The city walls constituted a place where people could ridicule, or complain about, the authorities."[52] At times throughout history, though, people who used graffiti to criticize those in power were punished for it. When Nero was emperor of the Roman Empire, for example, he imprisoned and even killed people who wrote negative graffiti about him.

The Berlin Wall, shown here, was a popular target for graffiti during the Cold War.

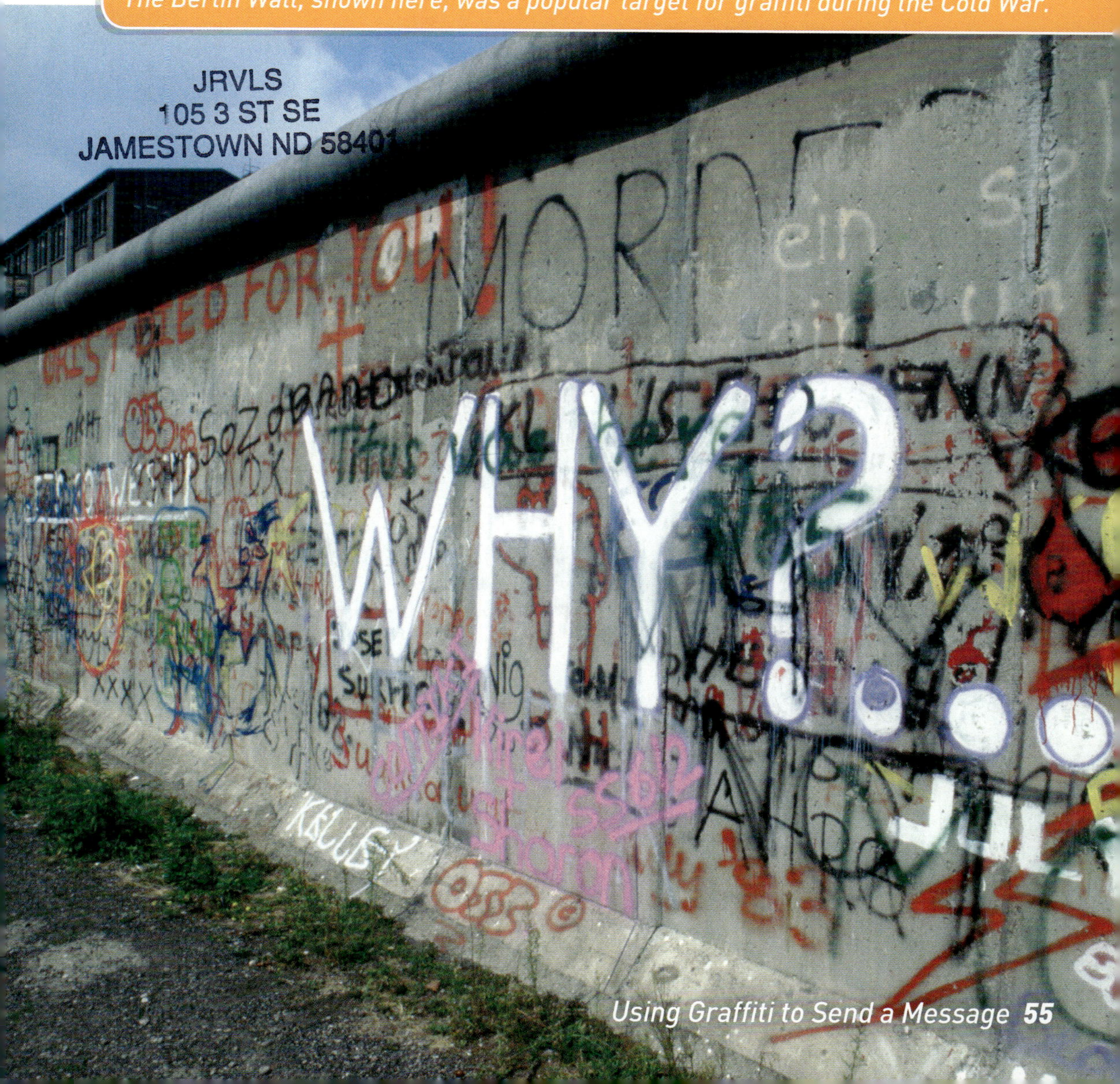

One of the most famous examples of political graffiti existed on the Berlin Wall, a structure that, from 1961 until 1989, divided Communist East Germany from democratic West Germany. The wall was 15 feet (4.6 m) tall and around 96 miles (154 km) long, and East Germany built it to prevent citizens from fleeing Communist rule. When it was dismantled in 1989, the entire length of the western side of the wall was covered with graffiti.

The most compelling topic among the messages written on the Berlin Wall was political freedom, such as the bold declaration "COMMUNISM STOP!" Famed New York graffiti artist Keith Haring contributed a 984-feet (300 m) long mural that showed linked figures in yellow, red, and black, the colors of the German flag. The linked figures in the mural symbolized unity. Today, the sections of the Berlin Wall that still stand are continuous targets for graffiti.

Similar walls also exist in Belfast in Northern Ireland. From 1969 to the mid-1990s—a period of unrest known today as "the Troubles"—violence between Catholics and Protestants prompted officials to build walls around the city dividing the Catholic and Protestant sections of neighborhoods. They are called "peace walls" because they were built to keep the peace. Now that the Troubles are over, the city has pledged to take down the walls. However, many of them still stand and are covered with political murals as well as messages of peace and love written by regular citizens and visitors to Belfast.

Political graffiti is still popular today, especially in Latin American countries where widespread poverty makes it difficult for many people to voice their opinions any other way. Latin American officials have traditionally been hard on the graffiti artists they catch, but as graffiti becomes more accepted by the mainstream, or popular, culture, attitudes are slowly changing. Juan Arellano, the Spanish-language editor for Global Voices Online, described what happened when a graffiti artist named Sose was caught by police in Iquitos, Peru:

> *[W]hile doing a mural on one of the streets of Iquitos, [Sose] was beaten and detained … as a criminal by members of the municipal police who took him to the police station, also taking away his "sprays" and drawing sketches. Following this, the Regional Director of Culture declared … his concern about the excessive force used against Sose and called for understanding from the municipal authorities as these artists help beautify the city.*[53]

Since many modern works of street art, even those with a political message, are colorful and beautiful, some authorities see them as a way to help people enjoy the city more. However, others still see them as vandalism and support strict penalties for people who are caught painting buildings without permission. This is especially true in the case of graffiti that sends a political message, particularly when it targets police or current leaders.

Political parties and elected officials who wield authority have also used graffiti to influence public opinion. In fact, one of the most powerful and historic uses of graffiti for political purposes was the way the Nazi Party used it to win control of Germany and persecute Jewish citizens.

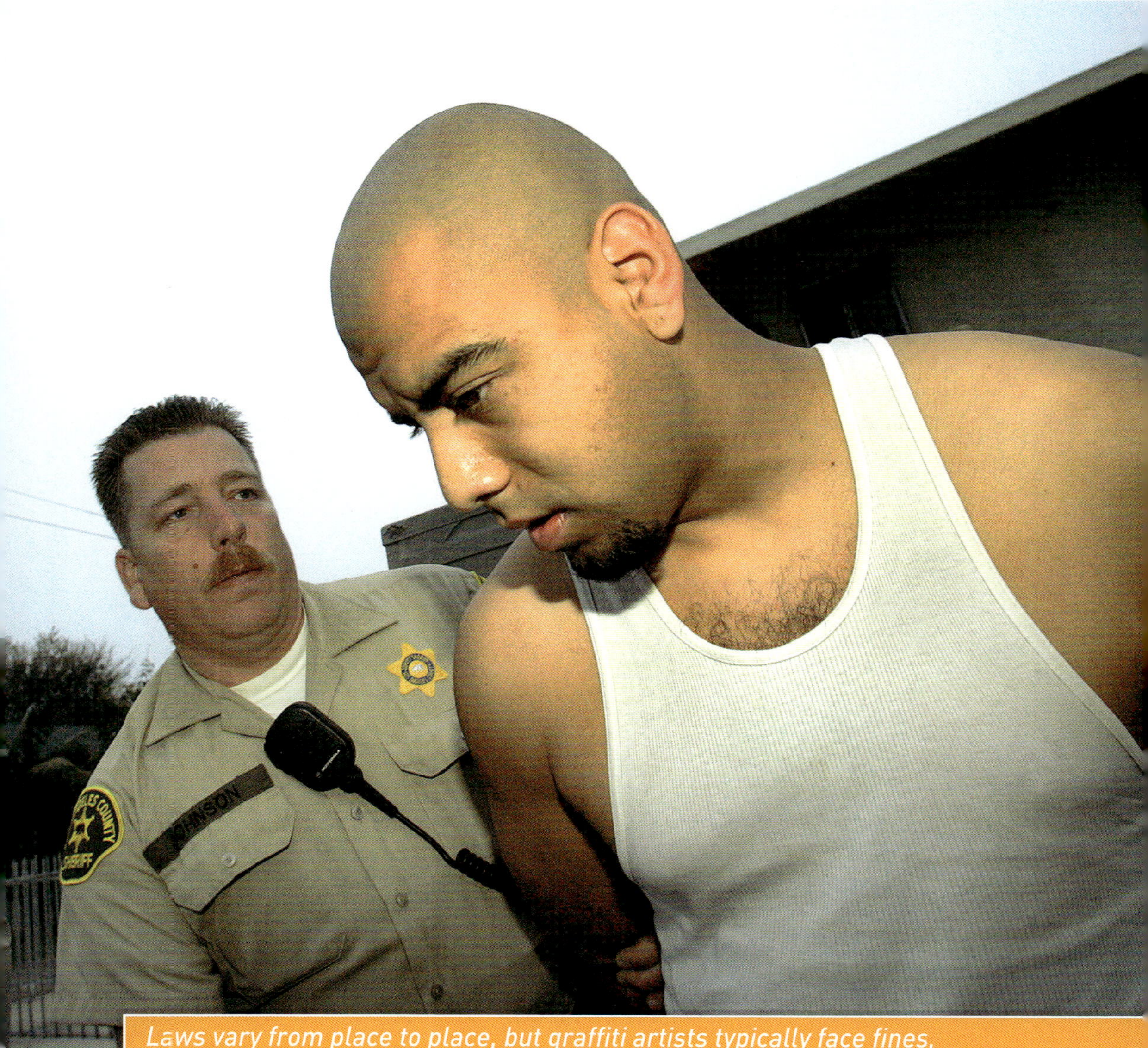

Laws vary from place to place, but graffiti artists typically face fines, imprisonment, and sometimes even violence if they are caught by the police.

Feminist Graffiti

Many female graffiti artists use their talents to draw people's attention to the issues women face in today's society. For instance, in Cairo, Egypt, graffiti "is increasingly used by Egyptian women to draw attention to issues of street harassment."[1] Artist Mirah Shihadeh has painted women blowing male figures away with a can of spray paint with the words "No to harassment" written alongside them in Arabic.

Another female artist who calls herself Princess Hijab has been painting niqabs—the veil some Muslim women use to cover the lower part of their face—on advertisements for women's products in Paris, France. The niqab is banned in France, so many people believed Princess Hijab's work was a protest against the ban, especially because hijab is the word for a different type of covering some Muslim women wear, which covers only the hair and neck, not the face or body. However, in an interview, Princess Hijab explained her motivations: "I chose the name 'Princess Hijab' because it conjures an exclusive person who operates out of sight ... It combines French Revolution with ethnic minorities."[2] According to the *Independent*, "She is out to 'hijabise' advertising by targeting cosmetic brands and well-known models, seeming to ask if hiding a face behind a veil is any different from hiding one behind make-up and air brushing."[3] These are only two of the many talented female street artists using their work to make a point.

1. Chelsea Hawkins, "21 Daring Women Proving Street Art Isn't Just a Man's Game," *Mic*, March 27, 2014. mic.com/articles/85809/21-daring-women-proving-street-art-isn-t-just-a-man-s-game#.iCSpSldKV.
2. Quoted in Matilda Battersby, "Rare Interview with Urban Artist Princess Hijab," *Independent*, June 16, 2011. www.independent.co.uk/arts-entertainment/art/features/rare-interview-with-urban-artist-princess-hijab-2297761.html.
3. Battersby, "Rare Interview with Urban Artist Princess Hijab."

Graffiti as Political Propaganda

German dictator Adolf Hitler wrote *Mein Kampf*—its title in English means "My Struggle"—while he was imprisoned in 1924 for treason due to his failed attempt to take over local government in Munich, Germany. Published after his release from prison in 1925, the book was a blueprint for gaining political power. In it, Hitler explained how his National Socialist (Nazi) Party could use propaganda to win political support. He cautioned that propaganda—ideas or statements designed to influence other people's beliefs—should be simply worded so anyone could understand its message.

He wrote, "Propaganda must always be presented in a popular form and must fix its intellectual level so as not to be above the heads of the least intellectual of those to whom it is directed. The art of propaganda consists precisely in being able to awaken the imagination of the public through an appeal to their feelings."[54]

Hitler's skillful use of propaganda helped him win political control in Germany in 1933, less than a decade later. Nazi propaganda appealed to people emotionally rather than intellectually. Hitler's powerful speeches were peppered with short, dramatic phrases such as "Deutschland über alles" ("Germany above all"), and Nazi public rallies were dramatic, entertaining events filled with loud music and colorful, waving flags that excited people. Hitler also chose the swastika as the party's main symbol. The bold, intimidating, crooked-cross figure was universally recognized and created instant identification for the party wherever it appeared.

Graffiti fit neatly into Hitler's vision of what propaganda should be because it is good at expressing short, simple messages. His followers often used it to spread Nazi beliefs. With paint, chalk, and other substances, they scrawled phrases from his speeches on public spaces throughout Germany. The Nazis also used graffiti to attack political opponents and Jews. The menacing swastika often accompanied graffiti propaganda or was drawn alone as a symbol of the party's growing power.

Most Nazi propaganda was anti-Semitic. In his speeches, Hitler blamed Jews for Germany's defeat in World War I and for its economic problems. Hitler knew this tactic would be popular because anti-Semitism had always been strong in Germany. Nazis scrawled, "THE JEW IS OUR GREATEST ENEMY, BEWARE OF THE JEW" and other graffiti on Jewish businesses and synagogues, and the swastika became the world's most powerful anti-Semitic symbol.

It was dangerous to criticize the Nazis, but in 1942, a group known as the White Rose distributed leaflets criticizing Nazi rule in Germany. The group was led by Hans Scholl and his sister, Sophie, who were students at the University of Munich. Members of the White Rose also used graffiti to attack Hitler. On the night of February 3, 1943, group members wrote "Freedom" and "Down with Hitler" on the walls of the university and other buildings. Unfortunately, Hans and Sophie were soon found with leaflets in their possession and sentenced to death for treason.

The Nazi Party was destroyed when Germany lost World War II, but the swastika survived as a powerful anti-Semitic symbol. In fact, it has become the most all-purpose graffiti symbol of hatred and is used to demean people worldwide on the basis of race or religion.

In 2016, when Donald Trump was elected president of the United States, some people used graffiti featuring swastikas both to support and oppose him. Some who claimed to support him spray-painted swastikas in public places, sometimes in combination with racist messages such as "Make America white again." In contrast, some people who opposed him used swastikas around images of Trump to make the point that they felt he was acting in a way that reminded them of Hitler.

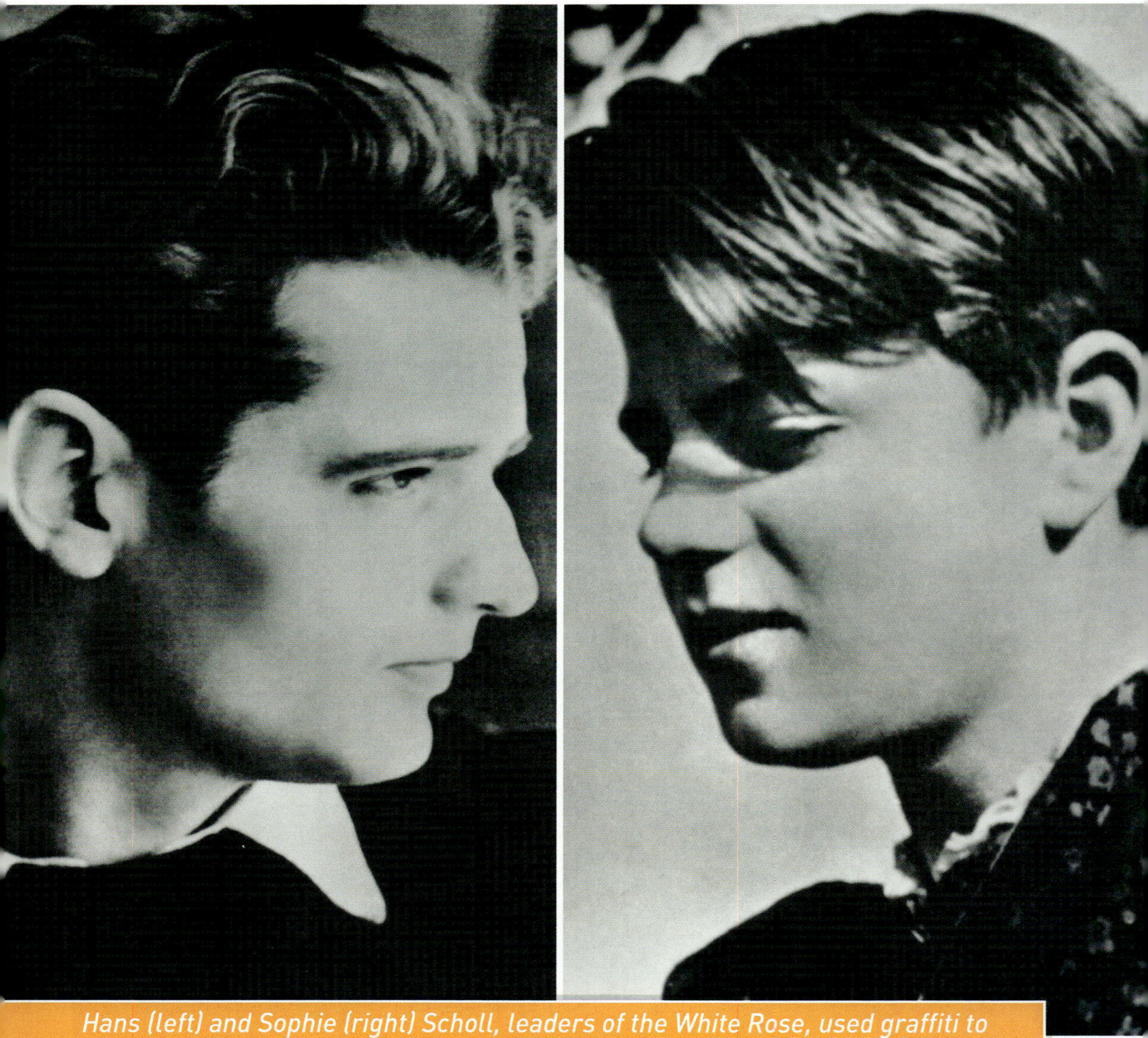

Hans (left) and Sophie (right) Scholl, leaders of the White Rose, used graffiti to criticize Adolf Hitler.

A Modern-Day Anti-Nazi Activist

Even in the present day, some people agree with Hitler's anti-Semitic views. Since the Nazi Party is no longer politically active, these people are called neo-Nazis ("neo" means "new"). In Germany, pro-Nazi graffiti and stickers are illegal, but officials are sometimes slow to remove them. For this reason, a German woman named Irmela Mensah-Schramm has made it her mission to remove pro-Nazi messages when she finds them. Since 1986, she has removed stickers and covered over hateful graffiti with hearts and other messages of love. She originally tried scrubbing the graffiti off the wall but found that covering it with her own graffiti had a better effect.

Sometimes people have called the police to report Mensah-Schramm, but she has said the police generally support her because she is covering graffiti that is illegal as well as offensive. However, in 2016, she was charged with damaging public property and fined 1,800 euros—which is equal to $2,016 U.S. dollars—when she painted over a slogan that was hateful but not obviously connected to the neo-Nazis. Many German citizens showed their support for Mensah-Schramm and her graffiti campaign by offering to help her pay the fine.

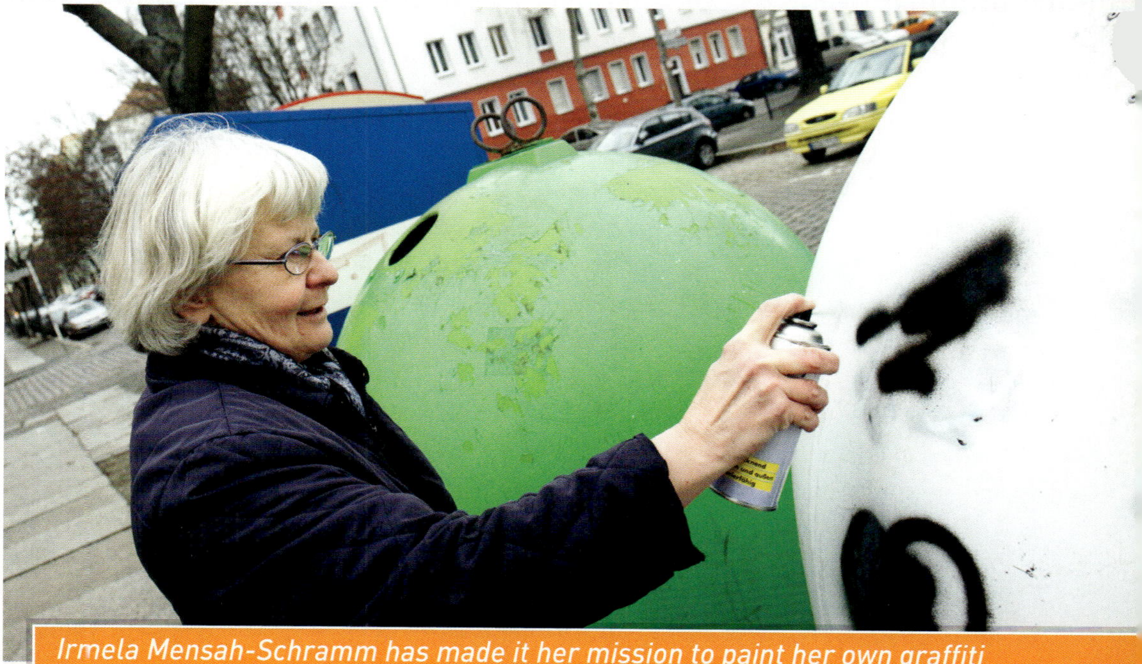

Irmela Mensah-Schramm has made it her mission to paint her own graffiti on top of pro-Nazi graffiti.

Using Graffiti to Spread Hatred

In April 2009, Orlando Diaz and his family returned from a vacation to find the interior of their Phoenix, Arizona, home covered with swastikas and other Nazi graffiti, as well as symbols of the Ku Klux Klan (KKK), a racist group that has persecuted black people for 150 years. On January 1, 2010, someone scrawled swastikas on the Kenesset Israel Torah Center in Sacramento, California. Just a few weeks later in France, swastikas were painted on a Muslim mosque. On February 1, 2010, swastika symbols and the letters "KKK" were discovered on doors and windows at Belleview High School in Belleview, Florida; their targets were African American students. After Donald Trump was elected president of the United States, the number of hate crimes in the country increased dramatically, especially against immigrants, Jews, and black people. Many of these involved graffiti written on personal cars or public structures. For instance, a Puerto Rican family found "the words 'Trump' and 'Go home' scratched into [their] car in West Springfield, Massachussetts,"[55] the news network CNN reported.

Incidents in the United States that involve such graffiti are considered hate crimes—criminal offenses in which bias against a person or group because of race, religion, sexual orientation, or ethnicity is the reason the perpetrator committed the act. The federal government and most states have separate hate crime laws with stiff penalties for such acts. Hate graffiti is one of the most common hate crimes, which also include other forms of vandalism, arson, verbal or physical assault, and murder. Thousands of graffiti hate crimes are committed each year in the United States against people on the basis of race, color, religion, national origin, gender, disability, or sexual orientation.

Much of this kind of graffiti is written by teenagers such as the two who, in January and February 2010, spray painted swastikas, racial slurs, and obscenities on property in Bourne and Sandwich, Massachusetts. Retired Bourne police lieutenant Richard Tavares said the graffiti was probably not motivated by hate: "We think they were just looking for attention. And unfortunately, now they're going to get it."[56] Although some graffiti is undoubtedly due to juvenile pranks rather than hate, graffiti experts warn that hate graffiti should be taken seriously because it can be an early warning sign that the writers may act physically against the targets of their graffiti.

The connection that exists between graffiti and possible physical harm to people it targets was behind the federal investigation of more than 200 hate crimes after Barack Obama was elected president of the United States on November 4, 2008. Many anti-Obama hate incidents involved graffiti, including some racist phrases four college students in Raleigh, North Carolina, sprayed in a pedestrian tunnel.

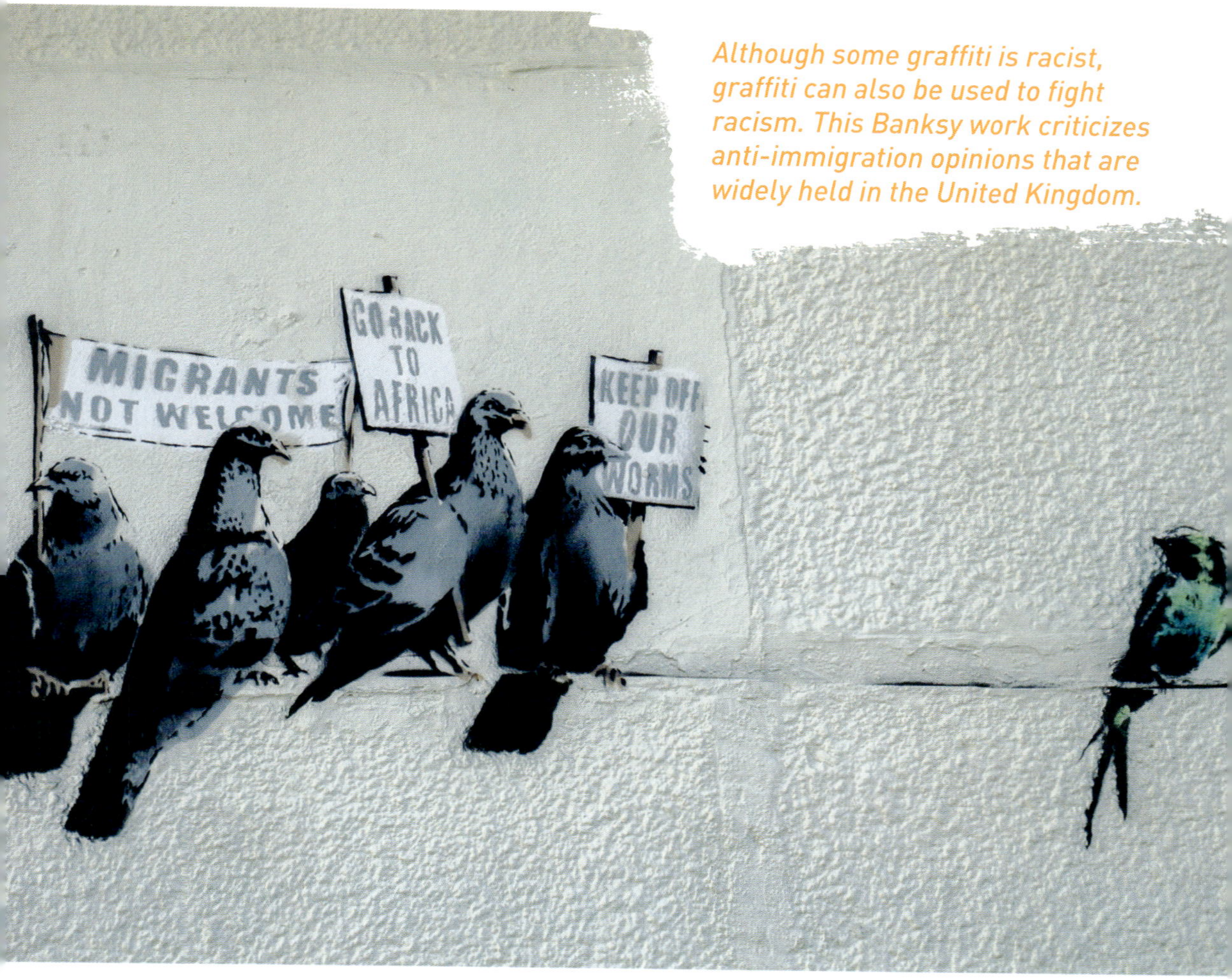

Although some graffiti is racist, graffiti can also be used to fight racism. This Banksy work criticizes anti-immigration opinions that are widely held in the United Kingdom.

The U.S. Secret Service, which guards the president, investigated the graffiti to make sure it would not lead to violence against Obama. Former Secret Service Special Agent Darrin Blackford said, "We're trying to be out there at the cutting edge of this [to protect Obama]."[57]

Although graffiti has been gaining acceptance as legitimate art, hate graffiti is a different matter. It is generally considered unacceptable because it targets specific groups of people with the intention of making them afraid. When street artists create political works, they are typically aimed at the politicians who make those decisions, not blameless victims, and they are generally not intended as threats. In February 2017, several news outlets reported a story that made clear how unacceptable most people find hate graffiti to be: When a group of strangers found swastikas and anti-Semitic messages written in Sharpie on the windows and posters of a New York City subway car, they banded together to remove them. Knowing that hand sanitizer would erase dried Sharpie, one of the people asked if anyone had any with them. Gregory Locke, one of the men on the train, wrote in a Facebook post, "I've never seen so many people simultaneously [at the same time] reach into their bags and pockets looking for tissues and [Purell.] Within about two minutes, all the Nazi symbolism was gone."[58]

Combining Faith and Art

Mohammed Ali—not to be confused with famous boxer Muhammad Ali—is a graffiti artist who was born in Bangladesh and grew up in Birmingham, England. Ali, who is known as Aerosol Arabic, often incorporates his Muslim faith into his works. In his blog, Ali wrote,

> *It was during my early twenties when I began to rediscover my faith. Questioning what life was all about, and where I was heading. Discovering Islamic calligraphy, and the fascinating parallels with graffiti ... As a graffiti artist I already had an obsession with the written word, so it was fascinating to discover how Islamic art was focused primarily on the written word, but instead of man's word, it was the word of God, written in intricate, elegant and fluid styles ... I became drawn to Islam, this was my solace. It gave me meaning, and Islam was now a big part of my life.*
>
> *Then September 11th happened. By this time I was experimenting with Islamic calligraphy and graffiti art. The two passions in my life were melded together, expressing my identity as an urban Muslim born and raised in the west.*[1]

Ali visited several U.S. cities in 2007, including New York, where he spray painted wall graffiti honoring nine children and an adult who died in a house fire. His classic-style graffiti included a verse from the Koran—"Verily To God We Belong ... TO HIM WE SHALL RETURN"—and the names of the victims. Creating the work profoundly affected Ali. He said, "Today changed me. Today I truly tasted the fruits of what art can bring. All I could hear was them [family and friends of victims] weeping behind me. This is spiritual, taking graffiti to the next level, reaching out to the community. Not just this community, but Muslims and Christians and Jews. This is something really powerful."[2]

1. The Art of Mohammed Ali Aerosol, "Spiritual Graffiti in the USA, an Emotional Rollercoaster Ride," blog entry by Mohammed Ali, April 30, 2007. www.aerosolarabic.com/2007/04/.
2. Quoted in Trymaine Lee, "Fire Victims Gain a Little Immortality Through Art," *New York Times*, April 19, 2007. www.nytimes.com/2007/04/19/nyregion/19mural.html?r=1& ref=nyregion.

Protesting War

People have used graffiti to oppose war in almost every period of history. During the Vietnam War in the 1960s, the phrase "Make love, not war" could be found scrawled on the walls of every big city in the United States. The Iraq War, which began in 2003, has also inspired a lot of graffiti. Xavier A. Tàpies wrote the text for a book of photographs of anti-Iraq War graffiti from many countries. He said graffiti gave antiwar activists an opportunity to state their views exactly as they wanted. Tàpies wrote, "[Graffiti] suddenly became one of the few uncensored channels of expression in an almost fascistic political climate. [A] brilliant bunch of artists used hyper-eloquent graffiti to give voice to the sense of fury [that many people] felt at runaway government."[59]

Written graffiti included messages such as "war is naughty," which was spray painted in Brighton, England, and the words "NO WAR" that appeared in red paint on the wing-like shells of the Sydney Opera House, one of Australia's most famous buildings. The opera house's chief executive at the time, Norman Gillespie, criticized the people who sprayed their message on the revered building. He stated, "While we respect the right of Australians to protest, it was a totally unacceptable way of doing it. To deface such a wonderful icon … It was an act of reckless vandalism, totally unacceptable."[60] The protest forced the opera house to institute new 24-hour security measures.

A lot of antiwar graffiti is much more artistic than mere writing. In Amsterdam, the Netherlands, a graffiti artist known as PJ spray painted "Make Jokes Not War" in English on a wall. The pink, orange, and blue bubble-style letters reminiscent of the golden age of graffiti appeared to float on blue and green clouds with a small black-and-white peace sign to one side. In Buenos Aires, Argentina, a replica of the Statue of Liberty with a skull face and holding a sickle instead of a torch depicted the U.S. symbol of freedom as the grim reaper of death. The art was done with a stencil, a graffiti method that enables artists to work quickly to avoid being arrested.

There was also graffiti supporting the Iraq War. In Boston, Massachusetts, someone wrote "GOD BLESS BUSH USA" near graffiti calling Bush a murderer. In 2005, someone who was allegedly a U.S. soldier wrote on a bathroom wall in Fallujah, Iraq: "Enjoy your freedom? Thank an American Marine!"

A favorite target of the antiwar graffiti was U.S. president George W. Bush, whom many people around the world blamed for starting the conflict by ordering the invasion of Iraq. Graffiti included Bush wearing a football helmet while clutching a bomb instead of a football in Cambridge, Massachusetts, and "BUSH" written in fat letters over a picture of a skull and crossbones in Rome, Italy. Anti-Bush graffiti was found in at least 26 countries.

Similarly, Obama and Trump have been the targets of graffiti. Obama had

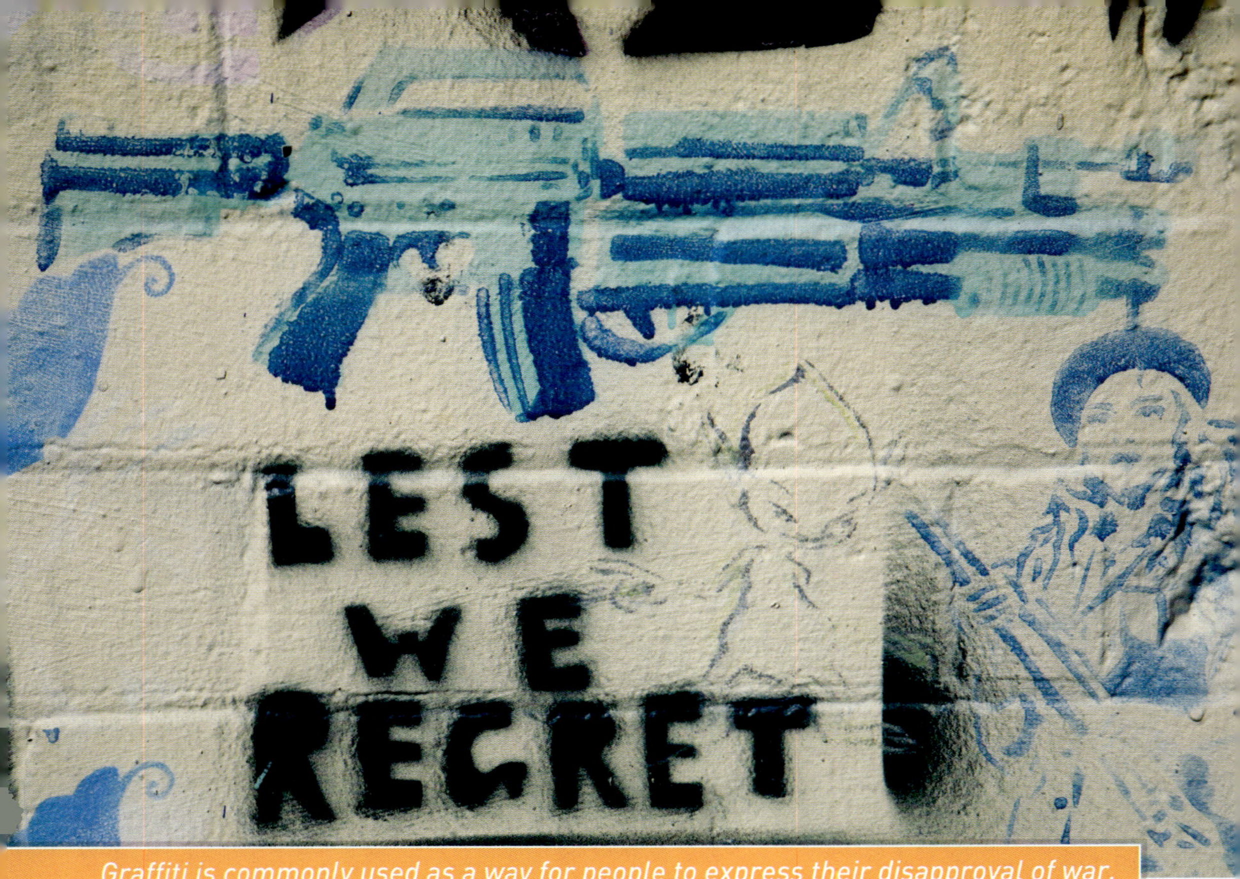

Graffiti is commonly used as a way for people to express their disapproval of war.

a higher approval rating than either Bush or Trump, but occasionally anti-Obama graffiti could be found. One example showed Bush holding a mask that looked like Obama's face, implying that Obama's policies were no better than Bush's. In Trump's case, in June 2016, someone spray painted the "mute" symbol on his star on the Hollywood Walk of Fame in Los Angeles, California.

Political graffiti, like other types of graffiti, can be found everywhere around the world, and over the past few years, it has grown in popularity and, with a few exceptions, has generally become accepted as art rather than vandalism. However, it is still illegal in many places, and some countries have especially strict penalties for graffiti artists who are caught painting public areas without permission.

CHAPTER FIVE

The Spread of Graffiti

Modern, artistic graffiti started in New York City, but it did not stay there. Writing graffiti and creating art are two activities humans have participated in for thousands of years, so it only made sense for the two to be combined. Graffiti art is a simple, effective way to send a message to many people at once no matter what language they speak, so it is no wonder graffiti quickly became popular around the world.

Zhang Dali, a graduate of Beijing's Central Academy of Fine Arts, brought graffiti home to China after seeing it in Italy. Graffiti then slowly spread to other Chinese cities such as Guangzhou, where Sic, a native of the city, founded Made in Guangzhou, China's first graffiti crew. Sic loved graffiti so much after seeing it on the Internet that she had to create her own. She explained, "It was crazy! You could do it anywhere. It wasn't necessarily beautiful but it was daring and brave."[61]

To many people, the fact that graffiti was still alive and well in the 21st century was amazing, especially in a nation like China, which was culturally isolated from current global trends for much of the 20th century and whose government still frowns on many types of individual expression, especially political criticism. In fact, most people had believed the graffiti craze would die out in 1989 after New York officials were finally able to secure the city's subway cars. However, that did not stop graffiti artists from pursuing their art elsewhere. In a statement about graffiti, Maze 139 boldly declared, "We may have lost the trains

... but we've gained the whole world."[62] It was not long before his prophecy was fulfilled. Modern graffiti soon began to travel the globe from its New York birthplace, and it became an accepted part of many different cultures in countries far different from the United States, such as China and Israel.

The Role of Books and Movies

One of the early catalysts that helped spread graffiti globally was the book *Subway Art* by Henry Chalfant and Martha Cooper. When Cooper visited Europe in 2003, many graffiti artists told her *Subway Art* had inspired them to start doing graffiti. "My favorite," Cooper recalled, "was the English writer who playfully shook his finger at me and said, 'You have a lot to account for.'"[63]

Graffiti got a giant global boost from hip-hop, which became popular in many countries during the last two decades of the 20th century. Graffiti became a major element of hip-hop culture because both developed about the same time in the 1970s in poor areas of New York and other big cities. When hip-hop culture spread around the world, so did graffiti. Clifford Joseph Price, who is of Jamaican and Scottish ancestry, discovered graffiti in England in the 1980s through his involvement in hip-hop music. Price said, "If I didn't learn graffiti the way I did—letter forms and outlines —I don't think I could do music the way I do now. It wouldn't be the same."[64] Price is well-known today as Goldie for both his graffiti and his music.

In 1983, *Wild Style*, the first hip-hop movie, glamorized graffiti by featuring legendary subway writers Lee Quiñones (Lee), Donald J. White (Dondi), and Sandra Fabara (Lady Pink).

Graffiti also began showing up in the backgrounds of movies and television shows such as *Welcome Back, Kotter*, a 1970s comedy about a high school teacher in a poor area of New York. English graffiti artist Mode 2 said that seeing graffiti in street scenes in the opening shots of *Kotter* made him want to learn more about it. Scottish graffiti artist Lyken Love—his tag, not his real name—also fell in love with graffiti the first time he saw it in 1983. He explained, "Weirdly, the first graffiti I ever saw was in six foot high skinny letters spelling out the words 'The Philadelphia Kids' and, even stranger than that, was the fact I was in Durban, South Africa at the time!"[65] Within a few years, Lyken Love was writing graffiti in his native Dundee, Scotland.

A major factor in graffiti's growth was the development of the World Wide Web. In the 1990s, graffiti websites became a powerful tool in introducing millions of people to the art form. New artists have gotten started doing graffiti just by trying to imitate work they have seen on the Internet.

Today graffiti exists in every corner of the world, although it is called by different names in other languages, such as *rakugaki* in Japanese, *pichação* in Portuguese, and *túyā* in Chinese.

Graffiti Creates Opportunities

Graffiti has always been especially popular with people who grew up in poverty because the materials are relatively cheap and the activity is free. Additionally, as graffiti has gained more acceptance in mainstream culture, it has become a stepping-stone to better opportunities for people who have a difficult time gaining success through more traditional methods. Many people who started off as graffiti artists have gone on to sell their artwork online, open tattoo parlors, take classes in art and marketing, and more. According to sociologist Gregory Snyder, "These kids refused the meager options presented to them by the larger society, and instead perfected extremely risky cultural pursuits ... Their success in this form eventually opened up other opportunities, and today those efforts are paying off, literally."[1]

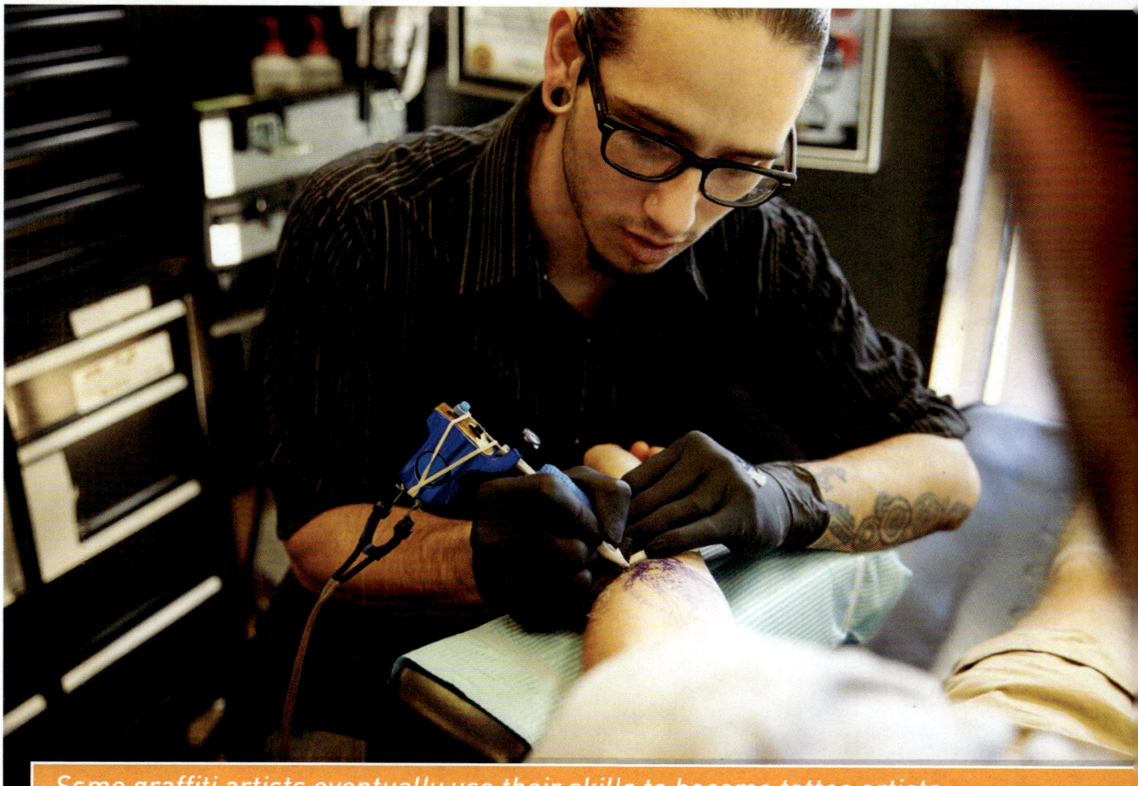

Some graffiti artists eventually use their skills to become tattoo artists.

1. Quoted in Sewell Chan, "A Sociologist's Look at Graffiti," *New York Times*, February 17, 2009. cityroom.blogs.nytimes.com/2009/02/17/a-new-look-at-graffiti-writers-lives/.

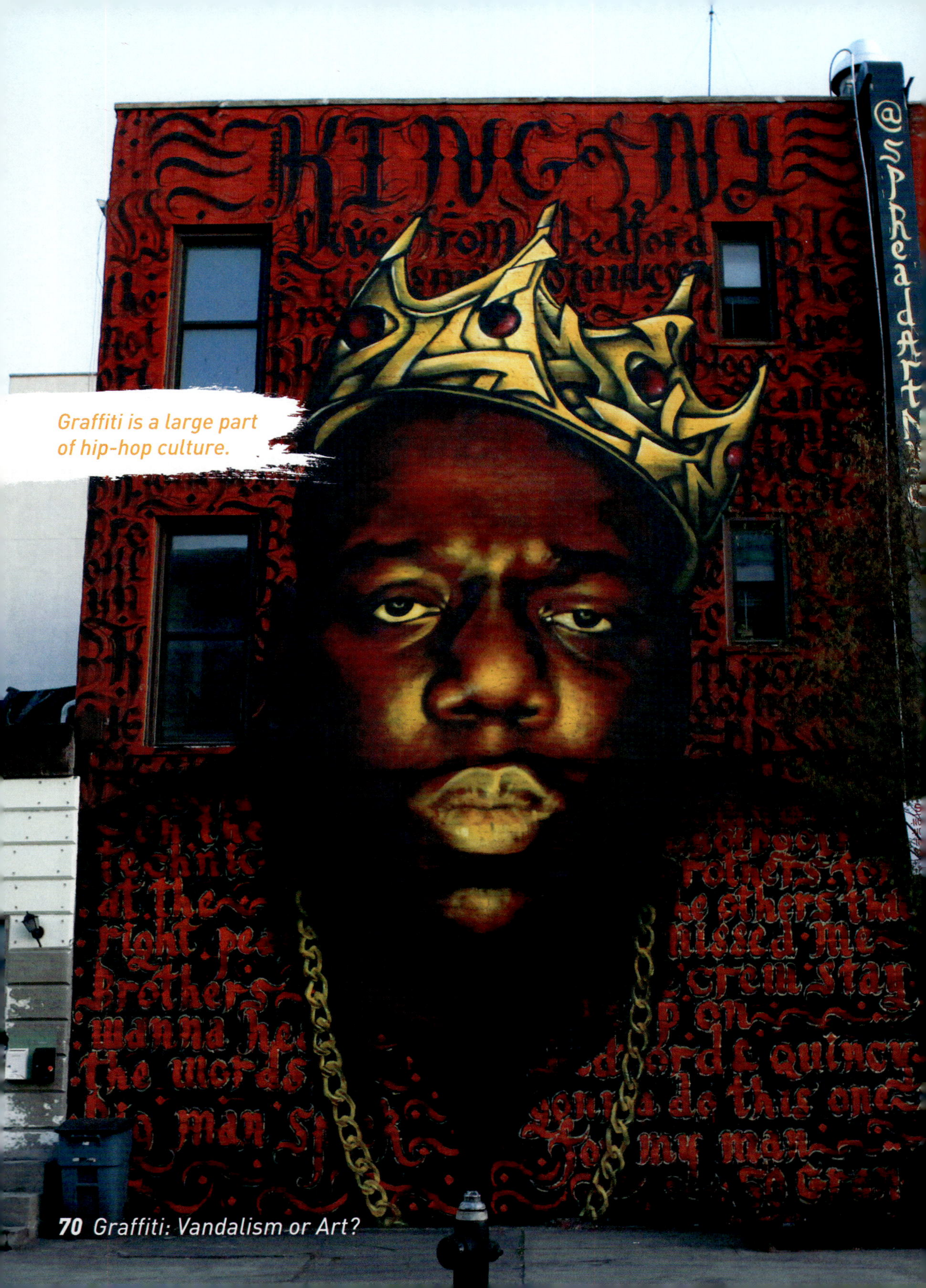

Graffiti is a large part of hip-hop culture.

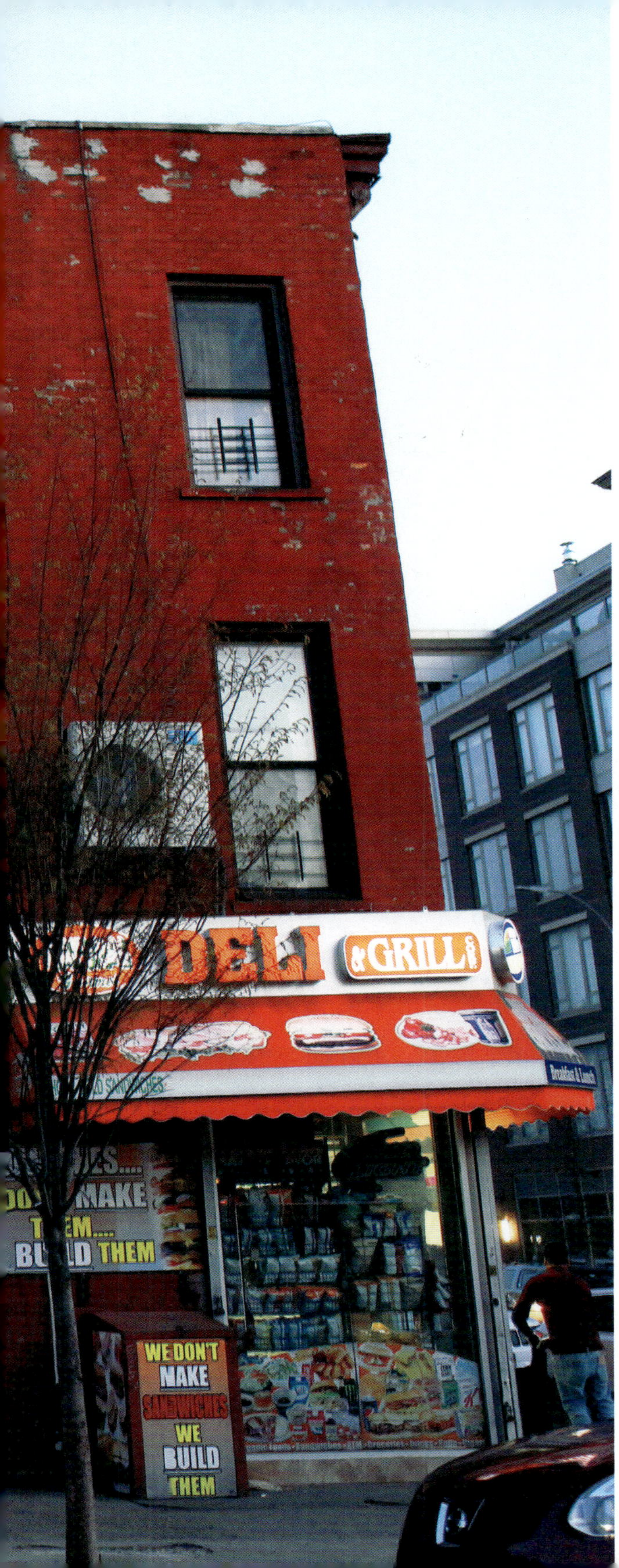

Friendship and Fights

The graffiti community has historically avoided documentation, generally to avoid the possibility of being caught and arrested, but also sometimes because its members enjoyed being anonymous. As graffiti has become more accepted, some have created their own websites to showcase their works, but before the widespread use of the Internet, this was obviously not possible. Because there is so little documentation, it is difficult to say for certain what the community was like when it was just getting started. During graffiti's golden age, some graffiti artists were likely friendly to one another even though they were competing to write the most tags or produce the biggest, most dramatic pieces. One reason for the closeness may have been that graffiti artists had common enemies—police and security guards who would arrest them for what they loved doing. They shared information about law enforcement activity aimed at stopping them. Mico explained, "Especially in the beginning, it was a guerrilla war. We had strategic maps of the subway system, of which yard or layup was hot or cooled off. We gathered intelligence info at the writers' bench. And if you got chased out at Coney Island that morning, you came to the bench and told everyone it was hot."[66]

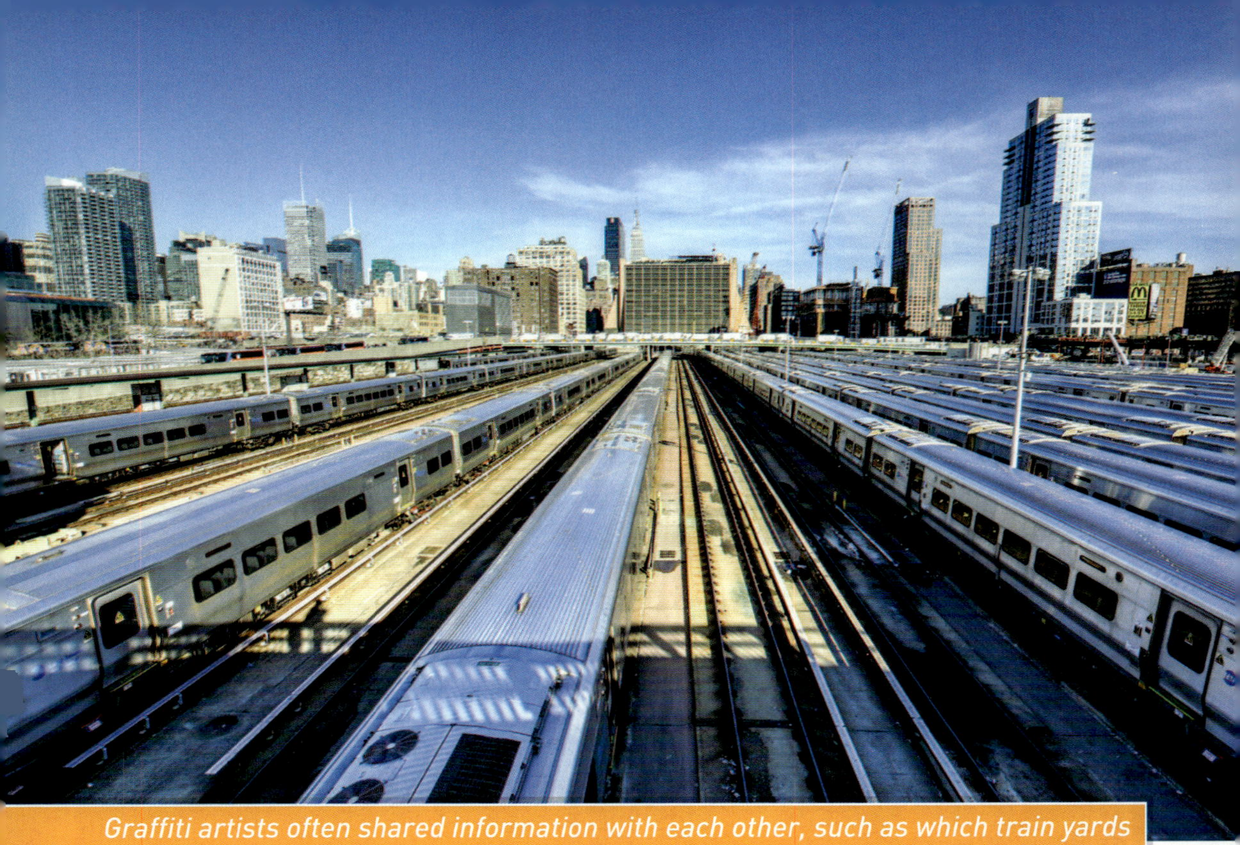

Graffiti artists often shared information with each other, such as which train yards the police were patrolling.

Graffiti artists gathered to share information, exchange techniques, or simply socialize at gathering spots they called either a "writer's bench" or "writer's corner." Some of their most popular meeting places were subway stations such as the 149th Street Grand Concourse subway station because the artists could watch their work travel past them while they talked—an activity they called "benching," which was how these areas became known as writers' benches. According to the website @149st, which documents the history of the graffiti movement, writers came to these areas "to meet, make plans, sign black books and settle disputes."[67] Skilled artists also shared their expertise with newcomers—everything from spray-painting techniques to how to evade security when getting into layups and yards housing subway cars. This educational process included becoming a member of a crew, a group of artists who worked together to produce graffiti under one tag. This was important to graffiti's growth. Fabara explained, "We're not taught [something like this] in school, this is nothing formal in a book or anything. It's all taught word of mouth, handed down master to apprentice. The only way to learn any of this stuff is to take up with a master or just somebody that knows a little bit more than you do and have them teach you the ropes."[68]

Graffiti Around the World

The book *Graffiti Planet 2: More of the Best Graffiti from Around the World*, published in 2009, features graffiti from around the world collected by Alain Maridueña, or "KET." In his book, Maridueña described the global graffiti scene. He wrote,

> *Walking the Streets of Berlin, São Paulo, Paris, and the Bronx [New York], it is easy to see that the aerosol art and writing movement is alive, well, and consistently growing. In such places there are [several] distinct schools of thought amongst graffiti artists. Some favor "bombing"—in other words the sport of tagging, which is all about getting our name around town quickly and prolifically. Another school, specifically in Berlin, has gone for an "anti-style" approach, where the names are created in simple designs reminiscent of New York, circa 1973. Another development has been the growth of the "street art" phenomenon, either where writers have turned to art that avoids the traditional use of letters, or art school students have decided that they too want to be part of the excitement of being public outlaws with their work.*[1]

1. KET, *Graffiti Planet 2: More of the Best Graffiti from Around the World*. London, UK: O'Mara, 2009, p. 1.

That sense of camaraderie helped thousands of people in New York join the graffiti explosion in the 1970s and 1980s. That sense of fellowship also existed after modern graffiti made its way to California in the mid-1980s. Fear and Dove, who began writing graffiti several years after its arrival in Los Angeles, found that established artists were happy to help them. Fear said:

> *When Dove and I met respected writers, they were cool with us and would teach us things … I schooled Dove a bit, but then he started excelling and learning different things that I never learned, so he started to school me a little bit. We learned from each other. [He] might learn some of the new tricks that people were doing and he'd get them down before I would, then I'd ask him "How … did you do that?"*[69]

Despite the overall level of goodwill among graffiti artists, there is some jealousy and competition. Gregory Snyder, a sociologist who interviewed many graffiti writers to learn more about their community, explained, "Beef [conflict] results in crossing out other writers' names, going over pieces, lots of stories about violence, and sometimes actual violence."[70]

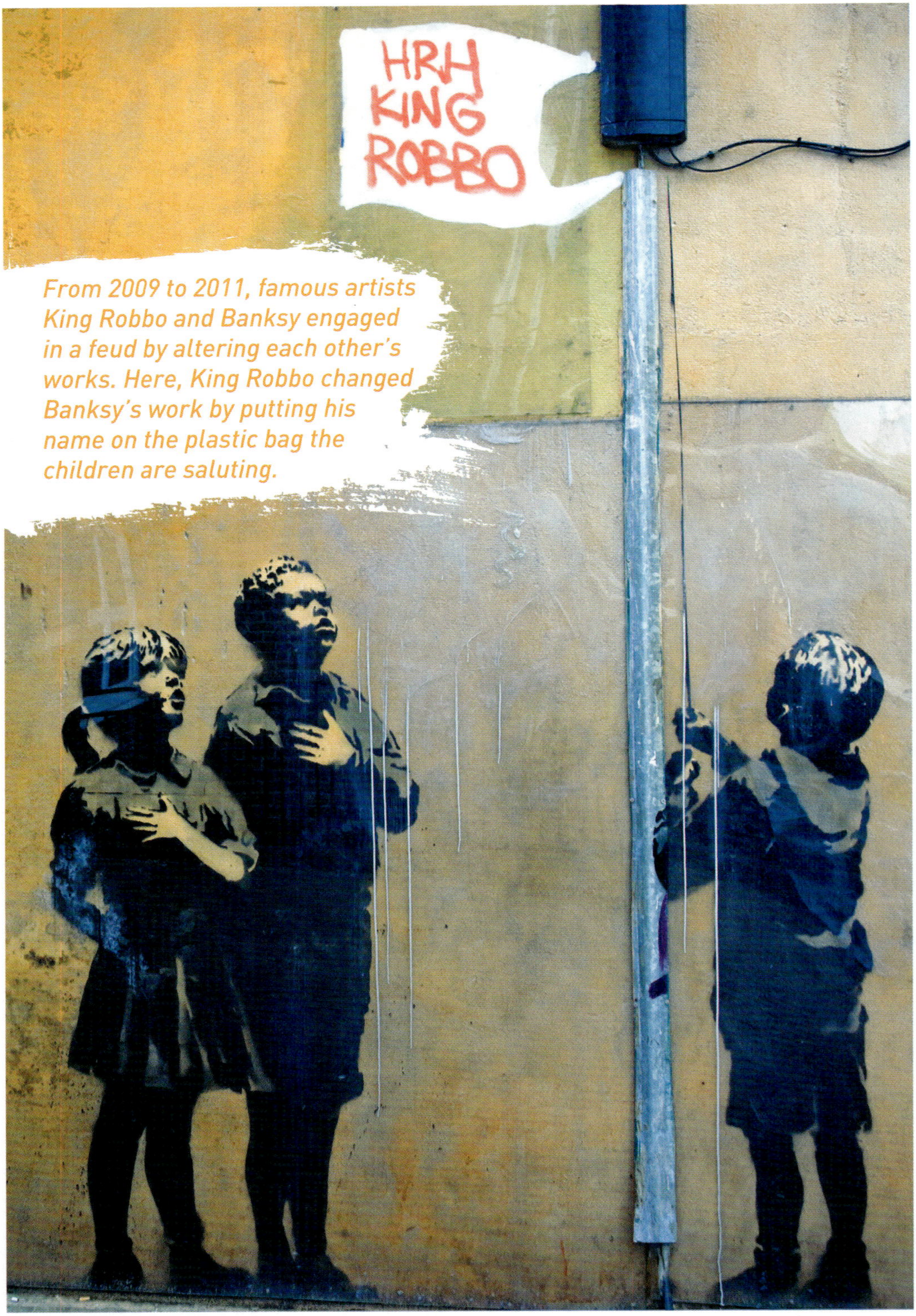

From 2009 to 2011, famous artists King Robbo and Banksy engaged in a feud by altering each other's works. Here, King Robbo changed Banksy's work by putting his name on the plastic bag the children are saluting.

Banding Together

Graffiti crews have often helped inexperienced artists learn to do graffiti. Educator Richard S. Christen explained,

> *The first crews were master groups of highly skilled and experienced writers ... The high standards and exclusivity of these crews created intense competition among those vying for membership as well as between rival groups. Beginners' crews and groups composed of writers at various levels of proficiency also surfaced. The Baltimore writer Deka became involved in one of these multi-level crews as a teen. Touched by "a fever" for graffiti at the age of ten, he regularly cut his high school classes to watch and draw with older, more accomplished writers who would critique his work and at times share letter models with him. Eventually some took him into their crew, where Deka assisted on pieces designed and executed by his mentors: "They took me on, and I just started doing characters and stuff like that cause they were doing heavy detail work," he recalls. "It's almost like an apprenticeship, they'd start you off with characters so you couldn't mess up the wall too bad."*[1]

1. Richard S. Christen, "Hip Hop Learning: Graffiti as an Educator of Urban Teenagers," *Educational Foundations*, Fall 2003, p. 57.

International Graffiti

In 1978, artist John Howard moved to Brazil, the only Latin American country in which the official language is Portuguese instead of Spanish. Brazil already had a lasting tradition of *pichação*, the country's name for written political graffiti. *Pichação* is considered different than graffiti or street art because it is about deliberate vandalization as a way to express anger. Howard introduced Brazilian artists to modern graffiti, which is now practiced alongside *pichação*.

Another important visitor was Barry McGee, who went to Brazil in 1993. McGee had created formal artwork to earn a degree in painting and printmaking from the San Francisco Art Institute, but he had also painted graffiti as Twist. His graffiti is distinguished by a trademark character of a male figure with sagging eyes.

McGee worked with many Brazilian artists, including 19-year-old twin brothers Otavio and Gustavo Pandolfo. Today they are world famous as Os Gêmeos—Portuguese for "the twins"—and they credit McGee with shaping their graffiti careers. They said, "Twist made an important visit to São Paulo in 1993. We learned so much from him, and the information exchange was very important to [our] work."[71] The twins, who live in São Paulo, were also tutored by Howard and other graffiti artists from around the world.

Their involvement in break dancing and hip-hop music had already led the Pandolfo brothers to begin doing graffiti in the late 1980s. Even before McGee's visit, they were writing their tag with latex paint, which is the most common graffiti medium in Brazil because it is cheaper than spray paint. However, with the help of foreign graffiti artists, the twins developed their graffiti talents and became known for complex pieces that often

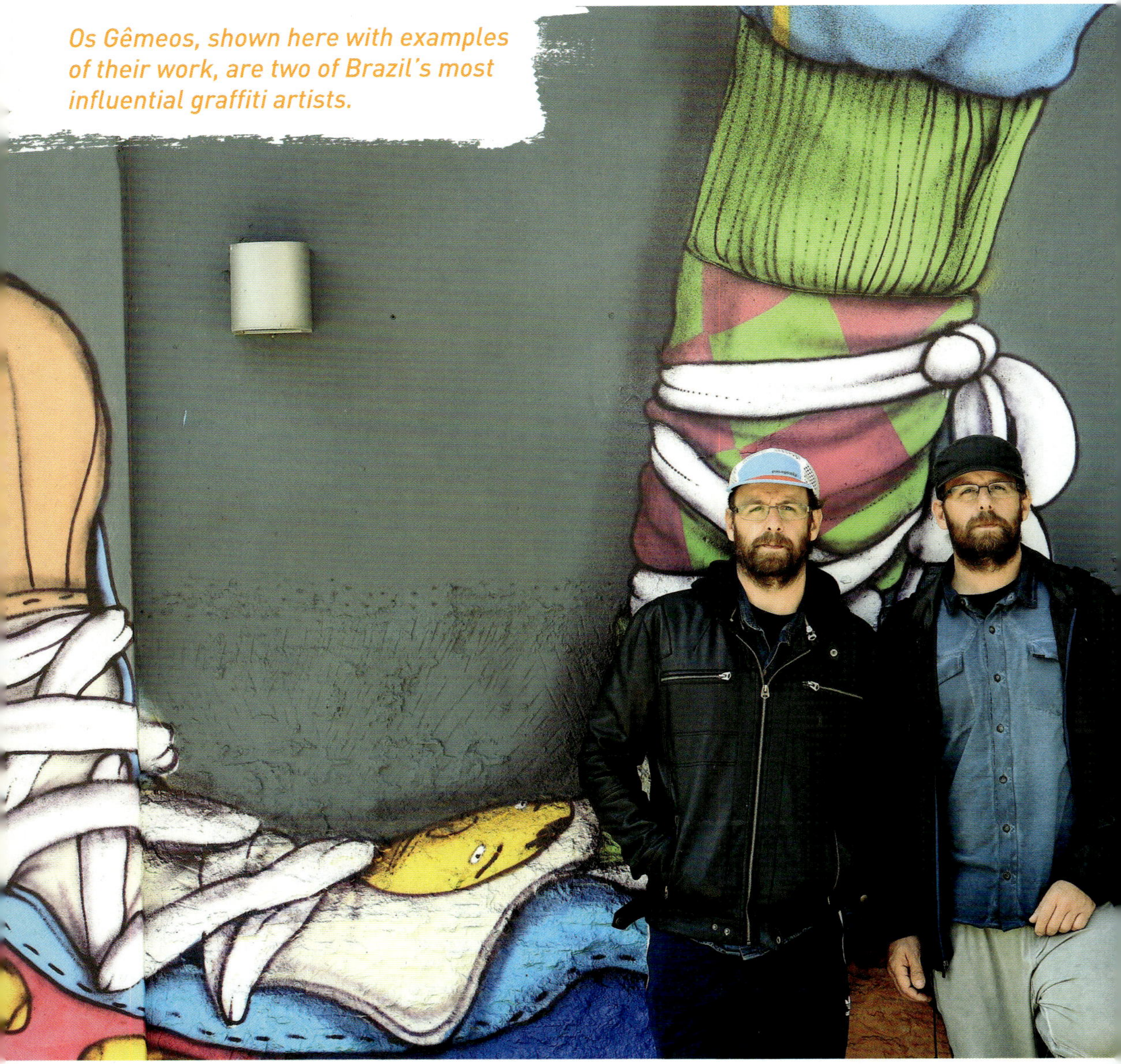

Os Gêmeos, shown here with examples of their work, are two of Brazil's most influential graffiti artists.

included one or more of their trademark yellow-skinned people. In paying tribute to subway art graffiti, they once painted a railroad car with one of their yellow-skinned characters lying down and extending the length of the car. McGee praised their graffiti, saying, "Their work ranges from lyrical and touching portraits of their beloved family to the gut-wrenching images of São Paulo's homeless, crippled, and forgotten. The brothers also mine Brazilian folktales, literature, and their own mutual family and world of fantasy for source material."[72]

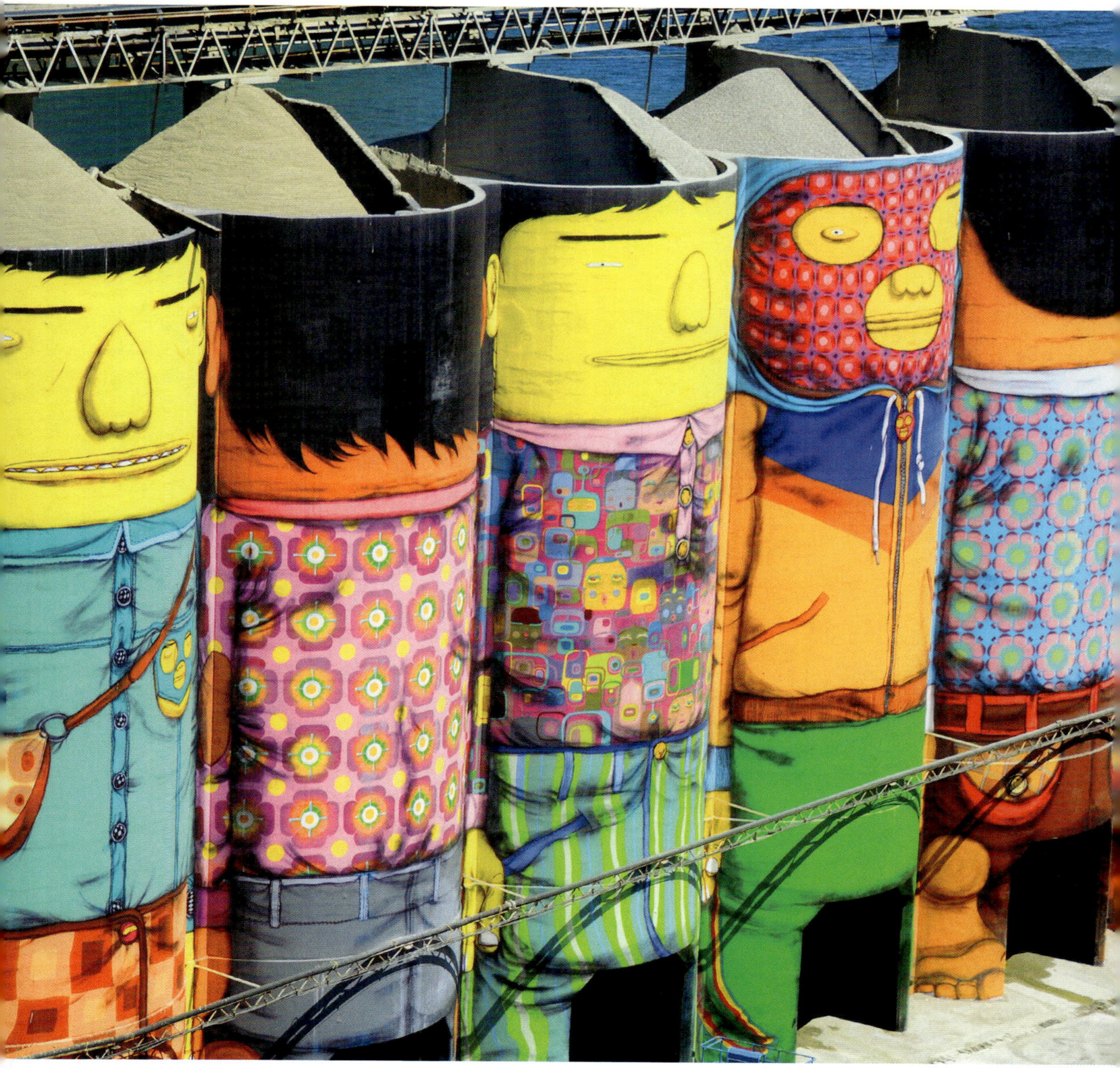

When the brothers are interviewed, they give united answers to questions because they consider Os Gêmeos to be a single art entity. "We are both part of one world: our world,"[73] they told one reporter. In his book *Graffiti World: Street Art from Five Continents*, author Nicholas Ganz credited the twins' fantastic imagination with their production of some of today's most interesting graffiti. He wrote, "Their pictures are reminiscent of drawings and illustrations from children's books and are plastered in every possible—and impossible—place."[74]

Ganz believes the mural-like works Os Gêmeos have created in Brazil and other countries have stretched the boundaries of graffiti in new directions. Os Gêmeos claim their graffiti evolved differently from graffiti in other countries because they knew so little about the art when they started. "We never watched anyone else painting … So we tried to discover how these things were done," they say. "We think we ended up discovering other things as a result."[75]

Brazilian culture undoubtedly shaped the way the brothers did their graffiti. Cultural differences have also shaped graffiti in other countries, and as a result,

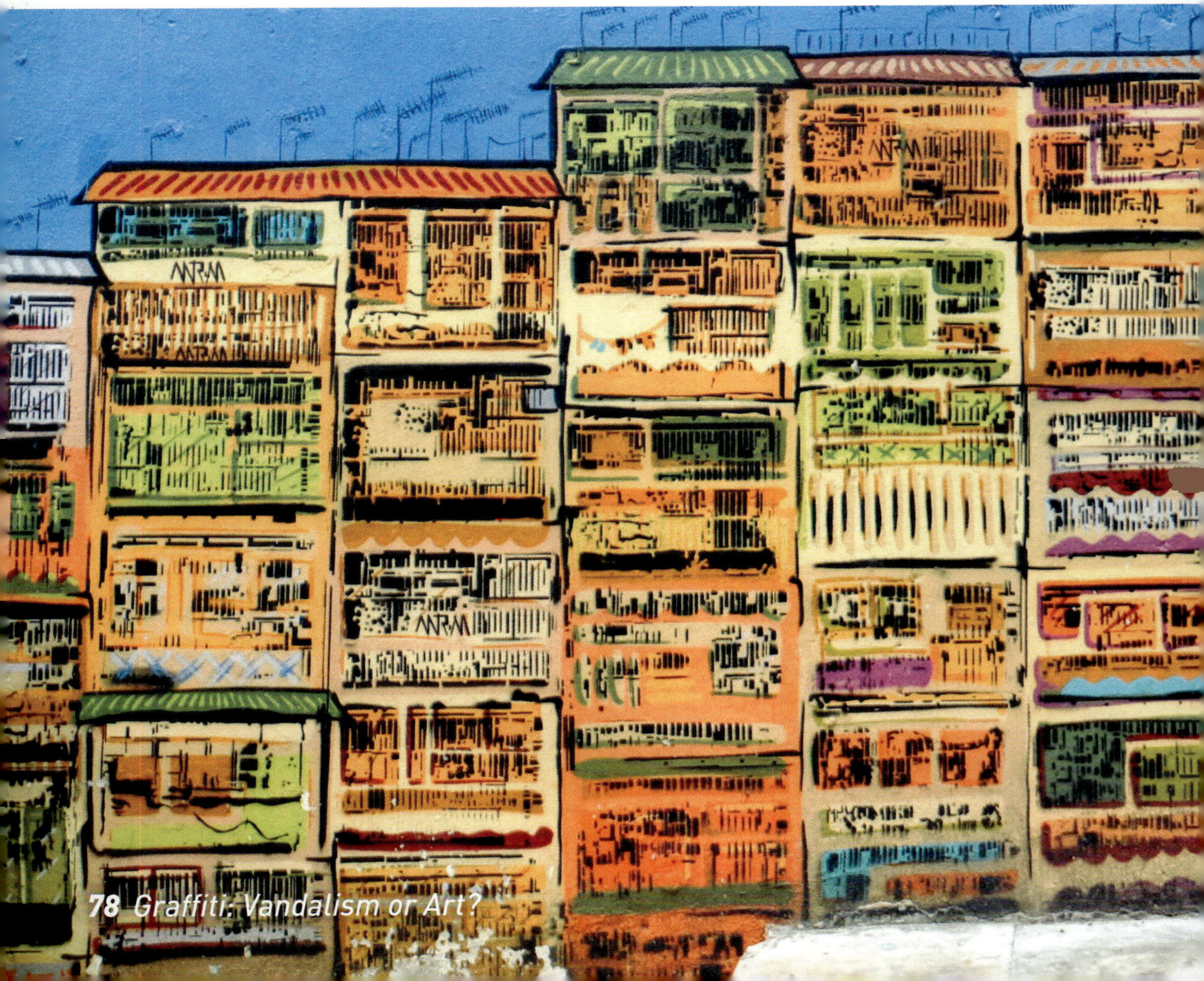

graffiti is a little bit different wherever people travel.

Because Communist officials tightly control individual expression in China, graffiti has grown slowly there. Chinese artists are not free to criticize their government. Beijing graffiti artist Seker noted, "There can't be political themes, and if there are, they must be beneficial towards the government or the [Communist] party."[76] That contrasts sharply with graffiti in countries where artists are free to criticize political figures and issues such as war and poverty. However, as long as the messages do not directly criticize the government and are not written on state-owned buildings, officials generally do not punish graffiti writers, even though their actions are technically illegal. In March 2014, a documentary called *Spray Paint Beijing* followed China's small graffiti community. The documentary's director, Lance Crayon, estimated the artist community contains no more than 200 people. ANDC, one of the artists featured in the documentary, said many Chinese graffiti artists work with big brands such as Red Bull and Louis Vuitton to create works that are partially advertisements.

The Chinese graffiti community is small but active. This graffiti in Hong Kong showcases their talent.

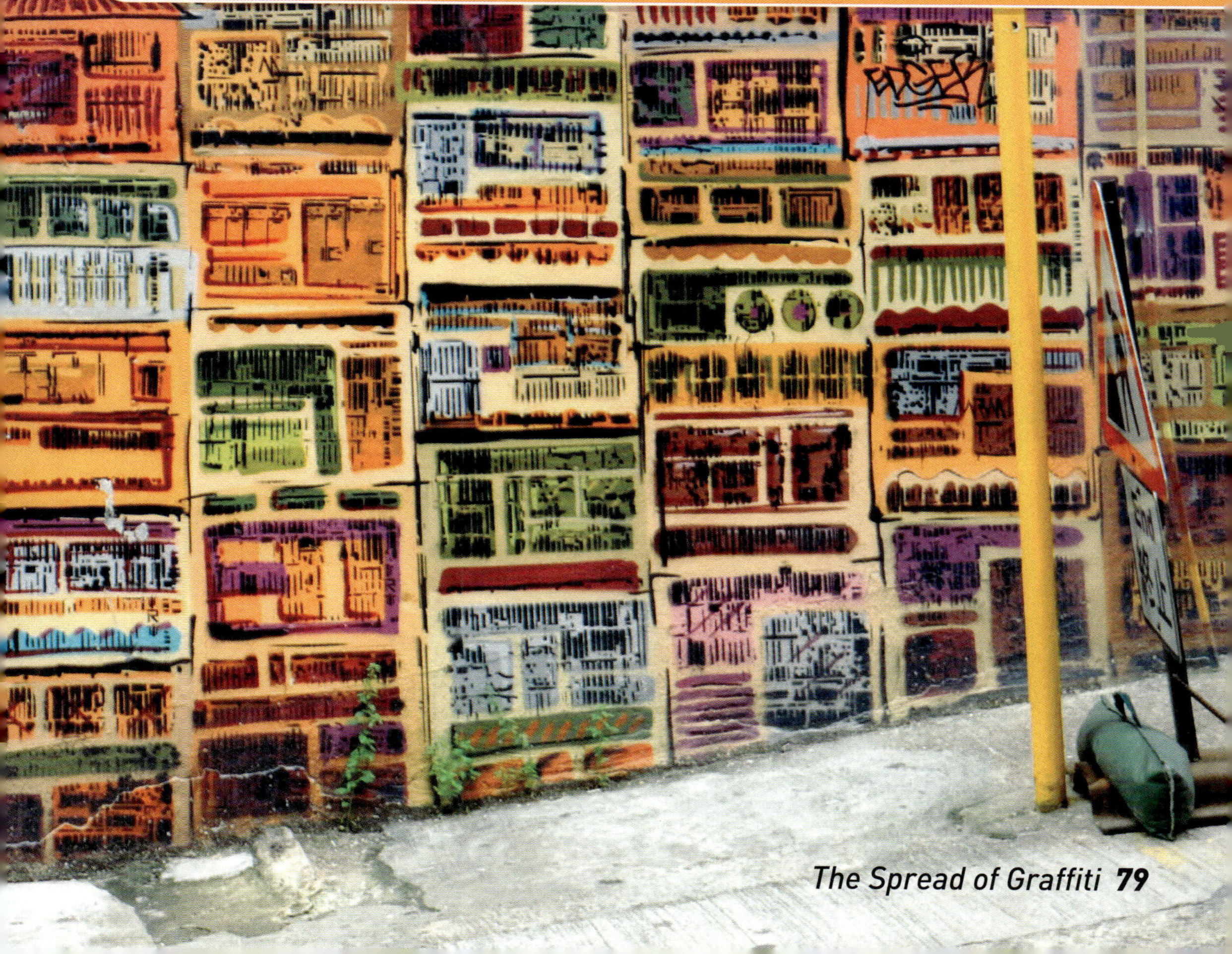

However, some types of graffiti are criticized by both the government and Chinese citizens. For instance, many people who climb Mount Everest, which is on the border between China and Nepal, leave their signatures, dates, and other messages to prove they were there. The Chinese government, in an effort to get people to stop doing this, threatened to shame these graffiti writers by publishing their names in the news. Additionally, the group that manages the Mount Everest base camp where most of this graffiti appears has considered setting up an area where people are allowed to write graffiti so tourists will stop doing it illegally.

Cultures of various countries have even led to new forms of graffiti. Brazil is famous for innovating *grapixo*, a hybrid form of graffiti lettering. This graffiti blends the thin, angular letters of São Paulo's *pichação*, which covers almost

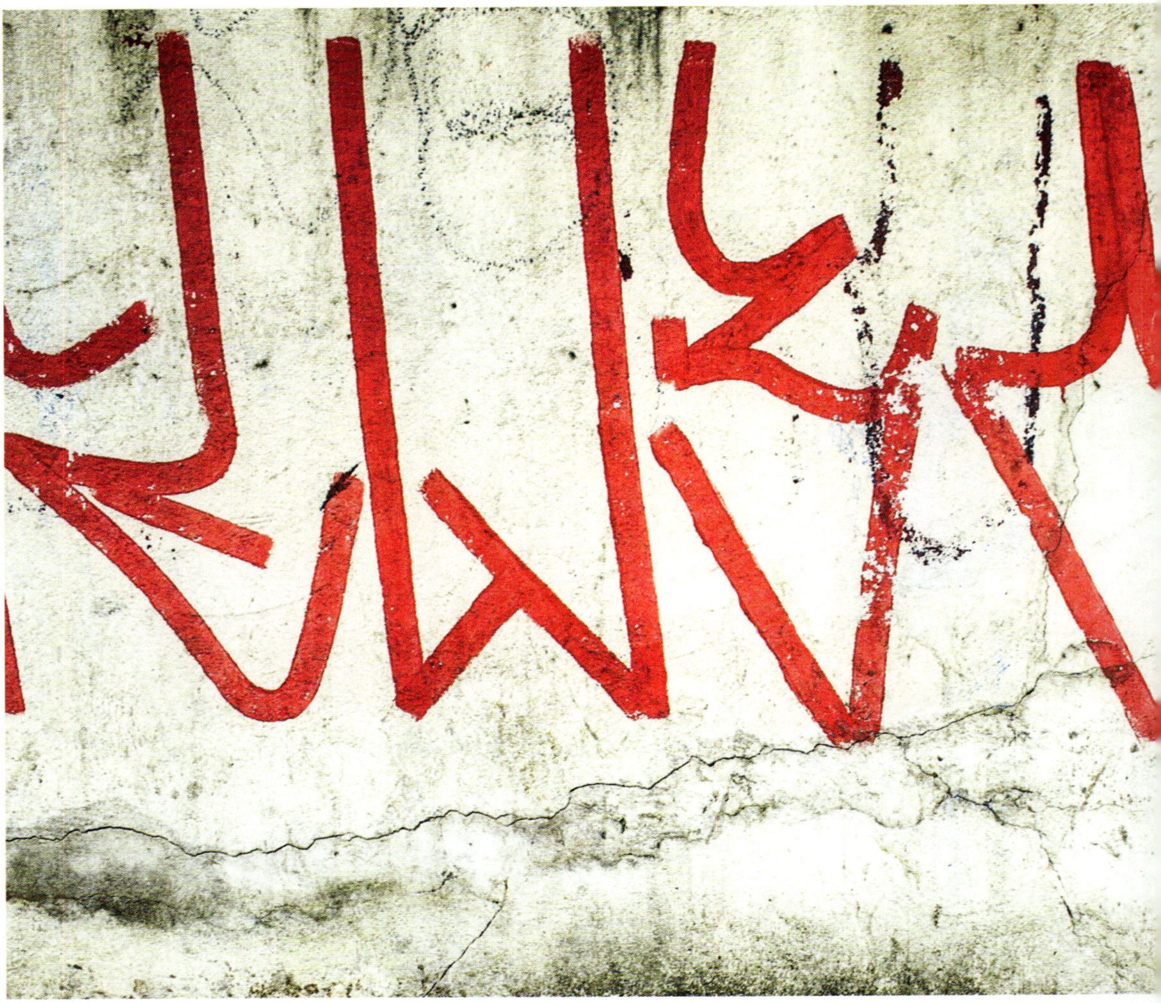

every bare space of every building, with the colorful, artistic lettering of modern graffiti that originated in New York. As such, *grapixo* reflects *antropfagia*, a Portuguese term for cannibalism that in Brazilian art means to borrow things from other cultures and adapt them to Brazilian culture.

Although graffiti has spread to nearly every nation in the world, it struggles to survive in many countries. A1one is one of only a few graffiti artists in Iran, a country in which such Western forms of culture are frowned on by a government dominated by Islamic religious leaders. A1one is also Iran's most famous artist, and he has exhibited his stencil graffiti in the United States. His work has inspired other Iranian graffiti artists, and in 2015, the *Huffington Post* reported on a documentary in progress about several of these artists, who are using graffiti to spread messages supporting freedom, peace, and love.

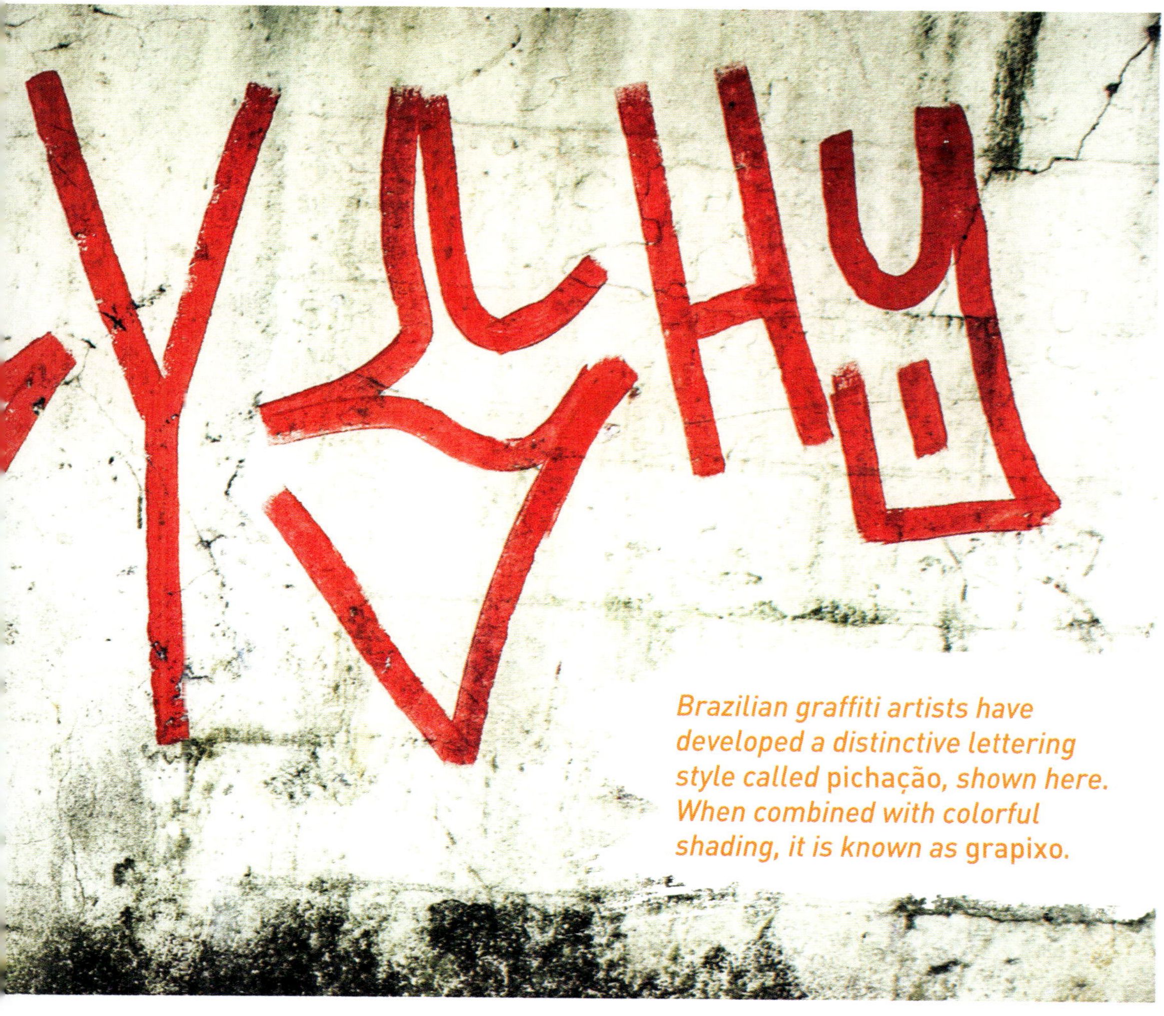

Brazilian graffiti artists have developed a distinctive lettering style called pichação, *shown here. When combined with colorful shading, it is known as* grapixo.

One year earlier, in 2014, the *Huffington Post* also reported that Athens, Greece, is becoming one of the biggest centers for street art and graffiti, largely due to Greece's economic crisis and high levels of unemployment. Some artists have used graffiti to comment on this situation, while others use it as an inexpensive outlet for their creativity. Other countries have also seen a rise in influential street art, including Poland, Spain, France, Italy, and Portugal.

Graffiti historian Cedar Lewisohn wrote that change should be expected because "the worlds of graffiti writing [are] constantly reinventing themselves."[77] This artistic evolution is happening not only due to cultural differences in various countries but also because of new media that artists are using today.

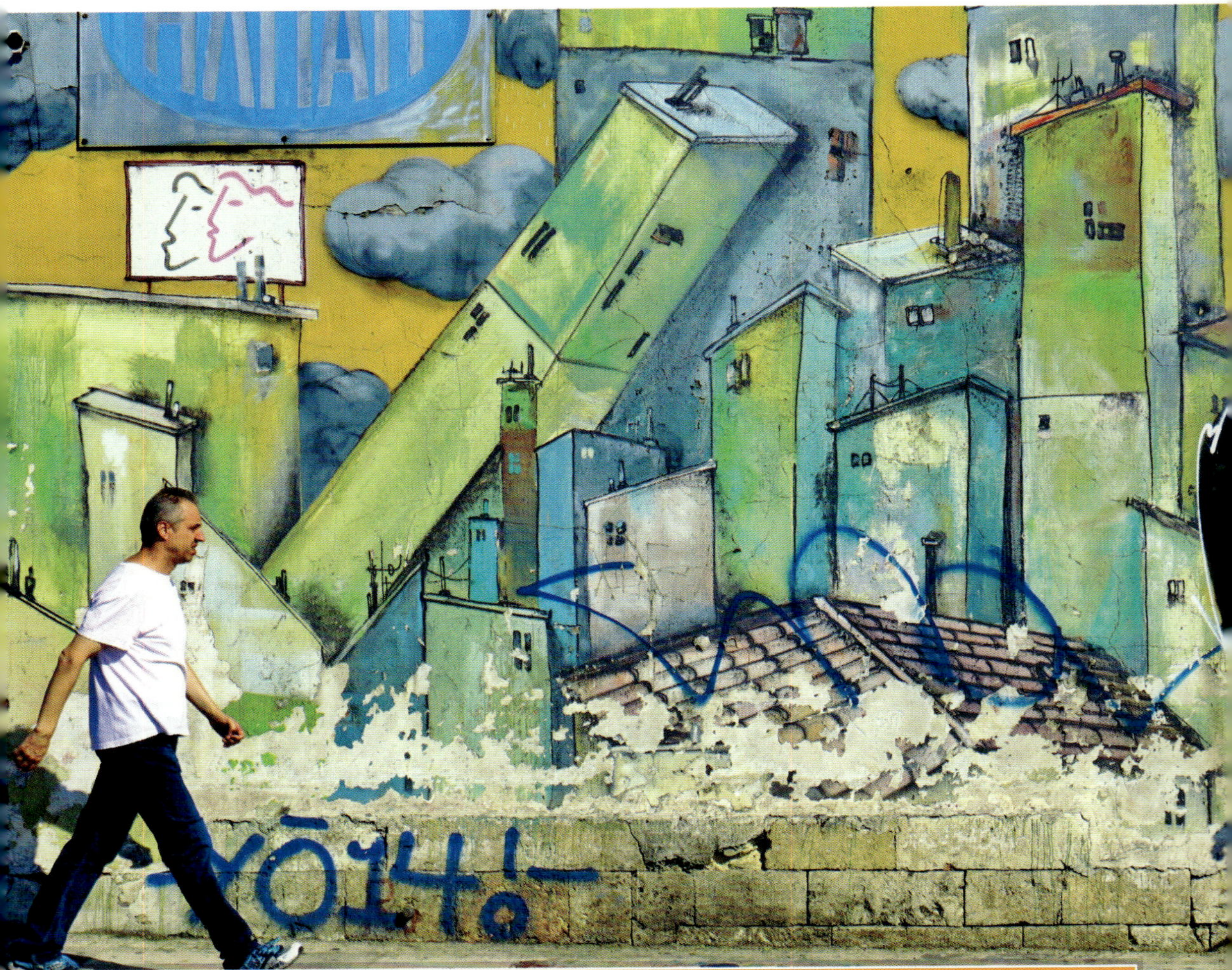

Athens, Greece, is becoming an important center for graffiti and street art.

Tools of the Trade

Graffiti artists use many different methods of creating their works. One tool is stencils, which are figures, shapes, and letters cut out of paper, cardboard, or other materials that allow artists to spray paint their work on various surfaces. They began using stencils because they sped up their work, which helped them avoid being arrested. Famed English graffiti artist Banksy said that when he was 18 years old, police nearly caught him while he was painting "LATE AGAIN" in silver bubble letters on a passenger train. Banksy said he got the idea for using stencils while hiding from police under a dump truck for over an hour, with oil from the truck dripping on him the whole time. He explained, "As I lay there listening to the cops on the tracks, I realised I had to cut my painting time in half or give up altogether. I was staring straight up at the stencilled plate on the bottom of a fuel tank when I realized I could just copy that style and make each letter 3 feet high."[78]

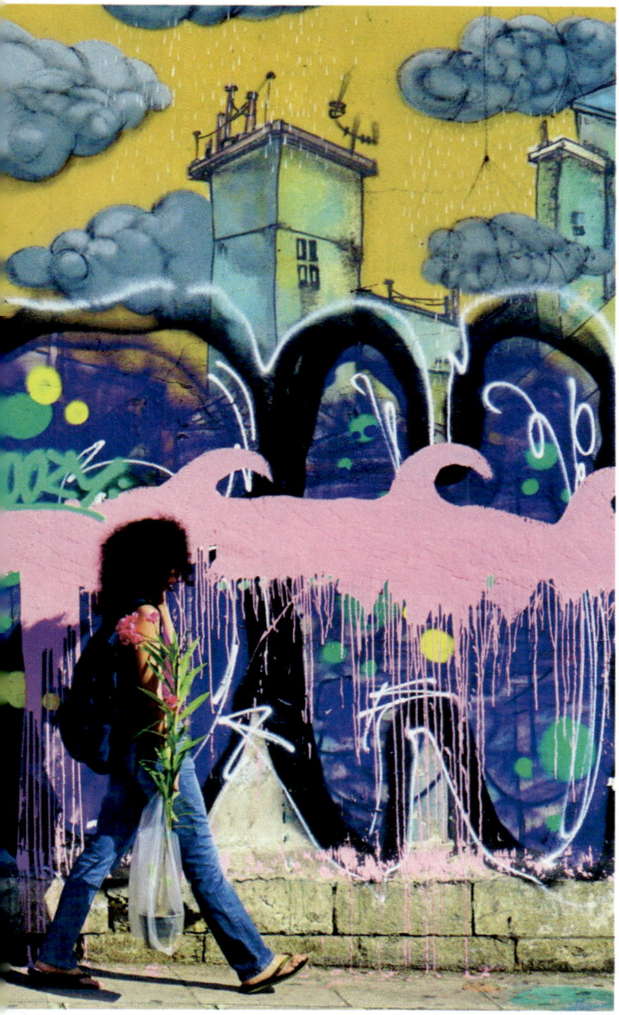

Stencils helped Banksy become famous. He decorated walls, bridges, and other flat surfaces in cities around the world with bizarre images of monkeys carrying weapons of mass destruction, policemen with smiley faces, and rats using drills and umbrellas.

Banksy, however, was only following in the footsteps of an earlier stencil graffiti artist from Paris—Blek le Rat, who was born in Paris in 1952 as Xavier Prou. He became famous in the early 1980s and acquired his tag for stenciling images of rats all over the city. Prou said he chose rats as a political statement. He explained, "They are the rebels of the city. They are evil. They live in groups. They steal food from the supermarkets. And Paris is full of rats. So it was a way of saying [be] careful where you're living."[79] Prou was influenced to pursue his graffiti career by the "Kilroy Was Here" messages U.S. soldiers had written during World War II, which were still present in Paris when Prou was growing up. He also saw examples of modern graffiti when he visited New York in 1971. Prou's work often involves political messages, and his stenciled images of people are so artfully done that they seem to come alive on the walls on which he places them.

Many graffiti and street artists use materials that have been around for years, but they find new and interesting ways to use them. One such material is wheat paste, which has been used for years to stick posters to the sides of buildings. Some artists use wheat paste to create paste-ups, or works that are similar to posters. Sometimes these works are legal, but if they are done without permission, they may be considered illegal.

Vhils, a Portugese artist, does not use paint to create his works; instead, he uses chisels and power drills to carve them directly into the wall. Joe Iurato of New Jersey paints images onto wood cutouts and sticks them in unlikely places. David Zinn draws on walls and sidewalks in Ann Arbor, Michigan, with chalk to create lifelike drawings. Chalk drawings are considered in many states to be a form of graffiti, so some people may be arrested for them. However, the rules regarding chalk can be confusing; a ban on chalk writing or drawing is considered unconstitutional if it is only selectively enforced, such as when several people "were cited and arrested for chalking anti-police department messages on various sidewalks … [They] alleged that the police department doesn't cite children who draw with chalk on public sidewalks, or adults who do the same 'when the messages are not critical of [the Metropolitan Police Department].'"[80]

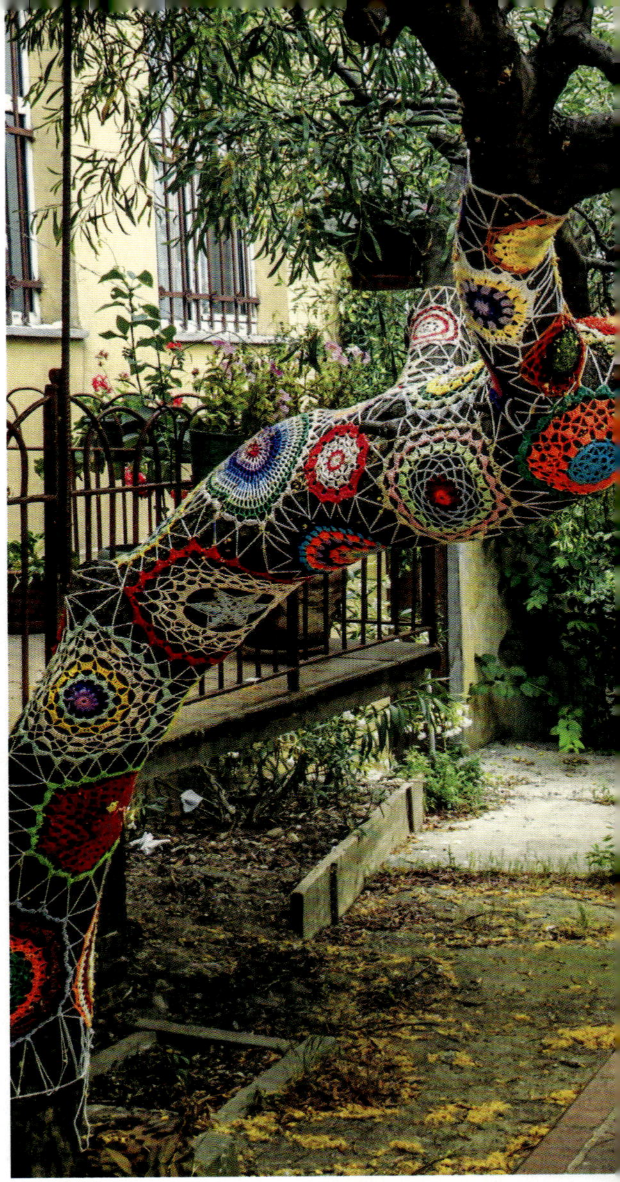

Yarn bombing, also called graffiti knitting or kniffiti, is the practice of covering trees, signs, benches, telephone poles, and other public items with knitted covers. London Kaye, a yarn bomber

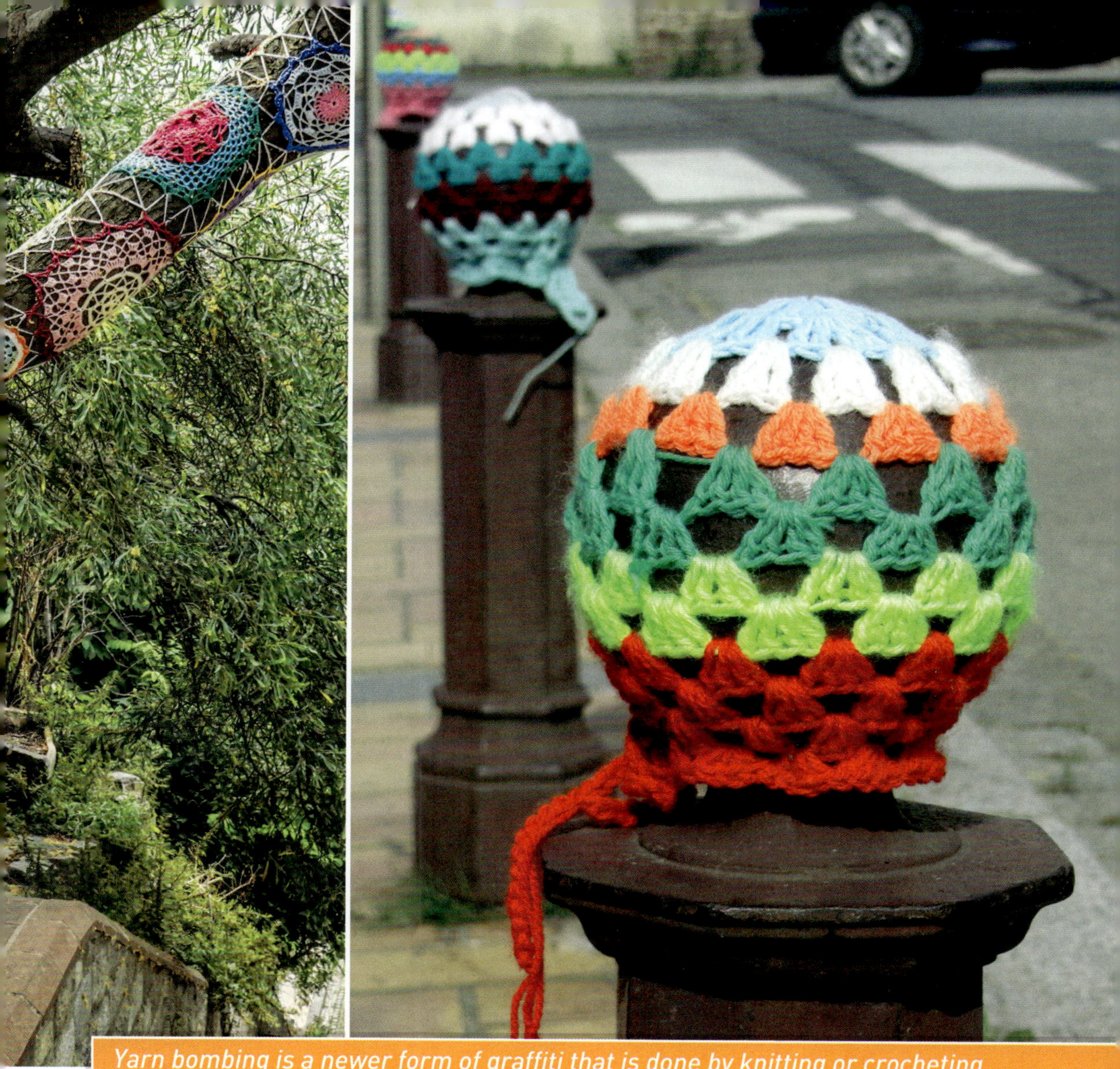

Yarn bombing is a newer form of graffiti that is done by knitting or crocheting covers for public objects.

based in New York City, said, "I love that I'm doing something that's so clearly a feminine craft, and putting it out there on the street with anybody else who's doing it. Street art's definitely done by mainly men."[81] Like chalk drawing, different places have different rules about yarn bombing. Some cities encourage it because they consider it to be beautiful, while others discourage it because people generally do not ask permission before yarn bombing. Attitudes toward graffiti have shifted over time, and it is increasingly difficult to tell whether a work will be considered legal or illegal.

CHAPTER SIX

Is Graffiti Really Art?

When graffiti was first becoming popular in Philadelphia and New York, even graffiti writers such as TAKI 183 tended to see their tags as vandalism. However, as graffiti has evolved over time and people have created unique and often colorful styles, it is increasingly viewed as art. Some people view graffiti and street art as the same thing, while others strongly believe they are different. Regardless, it is undoubtedly true that graffiti is becoming more mainstream, with art galleries showing graffiti exhibits and cities commissioning, or hiring, street artists to create murals as a way to beautify old buildings. Spray paint and markers, which used to be strictly regulated, can now be found in stores dedicated solely to selling graffiti supplies, and many graffiti artists showcase their works on their own websites.

Graffiti artist Barry McGee's gallery and museum art includes paintings and installations, works he creates by using different types of materials, objects, and media to transform a blank space into something artistic. His installations, which are often political statements on urban problems such as poverty, addiction, and the homeless, can include images painted on walls and other objects, such as liquor bottles purchased from homeless people. McGee may even scatter broken glass and punch a few holes in walls for added effect. McGee makes a living from such art but cares more about graffiti he does for free. He explained, "Every time I do a gallery piece, I have to put 110 percent more outdoors, to keep the street cred. It's the audience I'm most concerned with."[82]

Like many graffiti artists, McGee feels the pull of two worlds: the art world, which tends to accept his graffiti as art, and the general public, who sometimes see it as vandalism.

Some graffiti artists are proud to be displayed in museums, while others think it goes against the true spirit of graffiti.

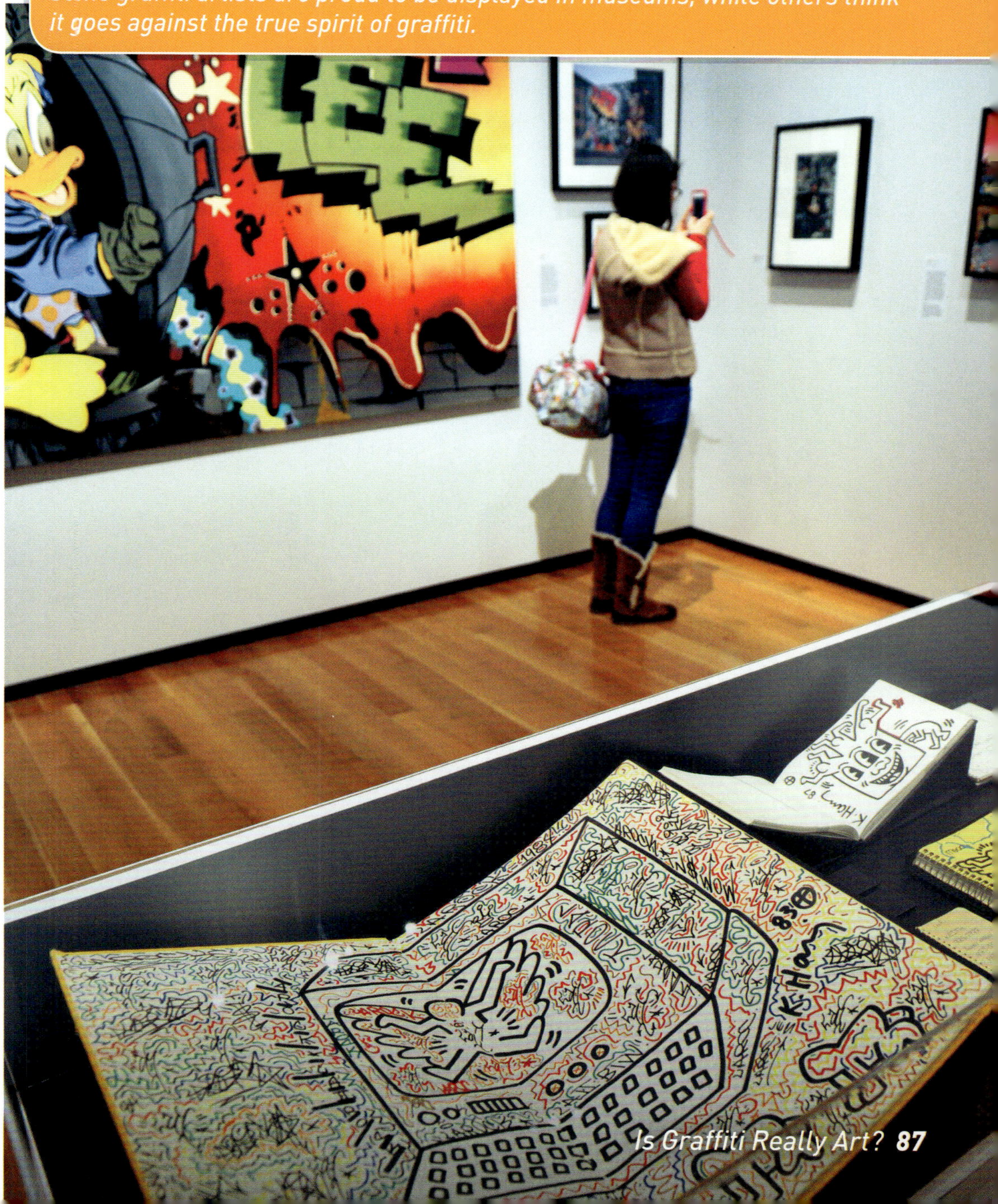

Choosing Murals over Graffiti

City officials have used many different methods to fight graffiti, from low-tech, chain-link fences to high-tech, graffiti-seeking intelligence services that utilize digital cameras and global positioning system (GPS) to find and analyze graffiti. Some business owners, such as Alberto Sanchez, hire graffiti artists such as Edward Mompeller, who goes by the name Playboy Eddie, to paint graffiti murals on their buildings. Sanchez owns Chico's Mexican Restaurant in Highland Park, California. He would rather have murals Mompeller paints, which depict Latinx history or a positive message for the community, than gang tags and obscenities. Sanchez claims the murals have helped keep negative graffiti off his walls because Mompeller is so respected by other graffiti writers that they leave his work alone.

This new tactic to curb unwelcome graffiti is used in countries around the world. In 2009, officials in Chesterton, England, set aside space in their subway system and encouraged young artists to paint whatever they wanted in an attempt to avoid having more negative graffiti placed there. Also in 2009, a nonprofit group in Montreal, Canada, hired graffiti artist Guillaume Lapointe to paint murals on buildings in the city's Notre Dame de Grâce neighborhood, including the Snowdon Bakery. Owner Abie Gmora said he is much happier having a baker wearing a white hat and some colorful abstract figures on his wall than scribbled tags that disfigure his business and have no connection to it.

Seeing Graffiti as Vandalism

In 1972, the *New York Times* published an opinion article stating that "subway graffiti are fast reaching what [a city official] has called 'the epidemic stage' here."[83] Since then, many cities in the United States have passed laws making graffiti illegal and making it harder for graffiti artists to obtain the materials they use to create graffiti, such as spray paint. Regardless of how creative or beautiful a graffiti piece might be, it is typically placed on someone else's property without the permission of the owner. While many people may not have an objection to the art itself and some may even appreciate it, many do not think that it is right that graffiti artists create their work in places that do not belong to them.

In 1990, Lompoc, California, passed its first anti-graffiti law to make it unlawful to deface property by graffiti, to sell spray paint to a minor, or for anyone younger than 18 to purchase or possess spray paint. However, two decades later, graffiti was still a problem there. Graffiti is considered a problem worldwide, even in places such as the remote South Pacific islands of Fiji. In 2009, town administrator Vijay Chand complained about obscene graffiti painted

Graffiti Art Moves Indoors

Some people admire graffiti so much that they are hiring graffiti artists to create murals in their homes. Ashley Goudie started out tagging trains in Victoria, Australia; as an adult, he started a business called KIL (Keeping It Legal) Productions, which creates custom graffiti-style murals. He is sometimes hired by parents to do murals in their children's bedrooms, even though he charges up to $2,500 for these paintings. One mother described graffiti as "an expression of personality and art, as long as you do it in the appropriate places."[1] Some people feel this defeats the purpose of graffiti, while others believe it is a good way to help graffiti shed its association with vandalism.

1. Carolyn Webb, "Artist Transforming Teenage Tags into Décor," *The Age*, April 4, 2016. www.theage.com.au/victoria/artist-transforming-teenage-tags-into-decor-20160403-gnx6gc.html.

on walls: "It is a menace in this town and we are trying to create awareness on the need for more civic pride."[84] Many people still find simple tags to be ugly and intimidating, especially when they are associated with gangs.

Some artists today paint legally on spaces provided by local governments or businesses or on media such as canvas so they can sell their work. However, many artists still enjoy the bandit aspect of graffiti that has always attracted so many people—the adrenaline rush artists get by doing something illegal without getting caught. As Chinese graffiti artist Sic admitted, "Some people prefer doing the legal stuff. It's more obedient but I like it out on the streets. I guess my heart's not yet at ease."[85] The love of doing something forbidden is so strong that some graffiti writers have said they would quit if graffiti were legalized.

Graffiti is not only considered an unwanted nuisance by many people; it is also expensive to clean up. Ironically, some famous graffiti artists have become victims of graffiti. TAKI, whose "TAKI 183" tag helped popularize graffiti in the 1960s, admitted in a 1989 newspaper story that the business he owned had been tagged repeatedly. He accepted the graffiti philosophically: "I am a victim. I painted it over and two weeks later it was all written up again. But I guess what goes around, comes around. It's justice."[86] The company founded by Edward Seymour, who invented canned spray paint, today markets a product to remove graffiti.

However, the graffiti that most people hate is graffiti that has no artistic merit, such as gang tags, messages expressing religious or racial hatred, and obscenities. Graffiti that is beautiful, colorful, or clever is often viewed quite differently.

Seeing Graffiti as Art

When complex spray-painted tags and subway aerosol masterpieces appeared in New York during the 1970s, many art critics, teachers, and other people who appreciated traditional arts, such as painting and sculpture, dismissed graffiti as colorful acts of vandalism. However, graffiti had its defenders even then.

In 1975, Hugo Martinez organized United Graffiti Artists so artists could display their work at a gallery. The exhibition drew a rave review for its "purity" from Peter Schjeldahl, one of New York's most influential art critics. The "purity" Schjeldahl praised was the fact that the graffiti was created by people with no art training, which means that it is original and unspoiled by previous ideas of what art should be. Also in 1975, English art critic Lawrence Alloway wrote about graffiti in *The Nation*, a respected magazine about politics and culture. Alloway admitted he enjoyed graffiti's "marks of individualism," "primitive energy," and the bright colors with which the pieces were done. He even commented positively on graffiti's illegal nature: "Though the writing amounted technically to vandalism, it's hard to object to the brilliant floralization of complete trains."[87]

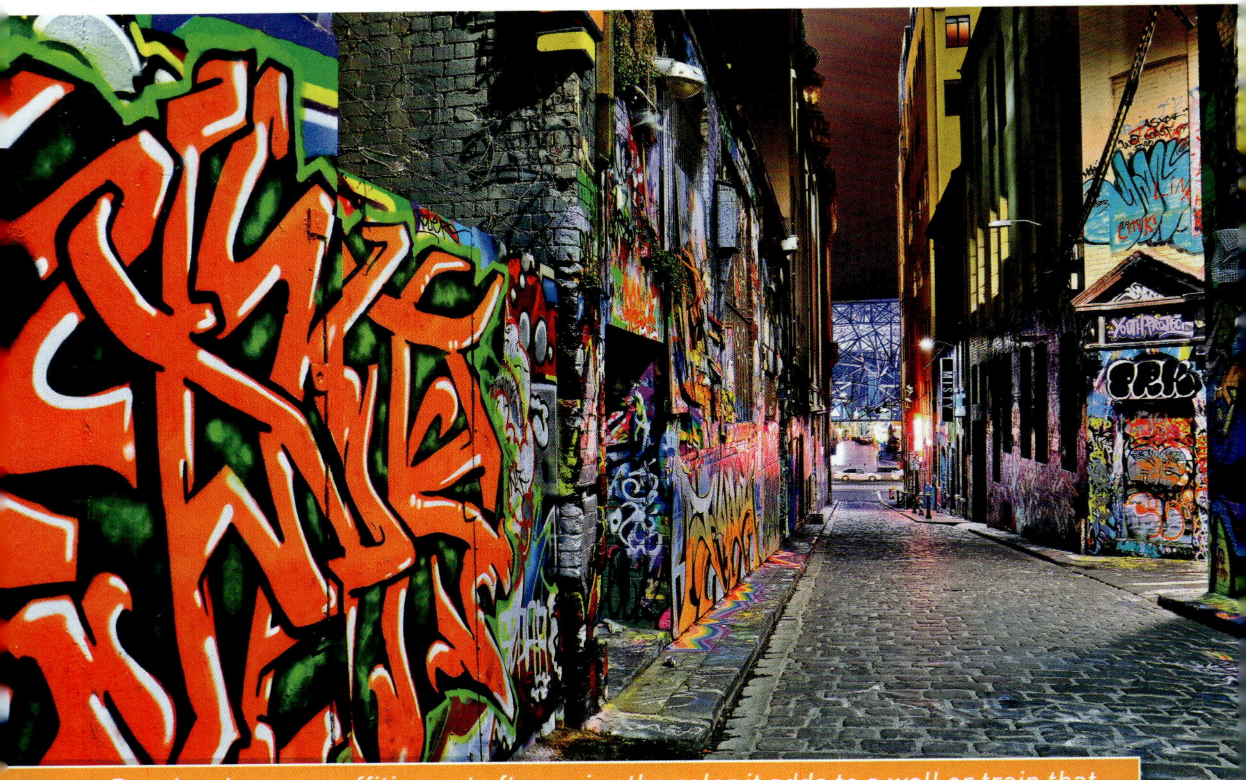

People who see graffiti as art often enjoy the color it adds to a wall or train that would otherwise be blank. They also tend to admire the artists' self-taught skills.

In the 1970s, many critics and art teachers were not accepting of modern graffiti because it did not fit their definition of what art should be. In the decades since then, though, that definition has expanded to include graffiti along with other, newer styles of artistic expression. Kenneth M. Lansing, a noted American art educator, fought for years for a new conception of art. He wrote, "Visual art is the skillful presentation of concepts and/or emotions (ideas and feelings) in a form that is structurally (compositionally) satisfying and coherent."[88]

Lansing's wide-ranging interpretation is generally shared in the art world today and no longer excludes graffiti. However, the acceptance of graffiti artists themselves began even earlier.

Graffiti Becomes Mainstream

Even as New York City officials in the 1980s were denying artists the canvases they wanted for their artwork by tightening security on subway cars, the artists themselves were becoming celebrities because of movies and other media that featured them. Artists such as Lady Pink, Jean-Michel Basquiat, Keith Haring, Lee Quiñones, Dondi, Doze, Fab 5 Freddy, and Futura used their new fame to sell paintings on canvas and other artwork. However, according to Lady Pink, many artists found it difficult to handle their new status. She said,

> *At night, we're lurking round in the shadows, trying to evade the police, and the next day, you have a bunch of rich people patting you on the back and giving you wads of money, and telling you, "Great work, wonderful." It was a bit surreal, dressing like a little bum, all dirty and disgusting, and the next day in high heels and a silk dress to a party.*[89]

Some graffiti artists refused to do art that could be sold in galleries because they believed it would disgrace graffiti's original illegal nature. However, most were happy to have the chance to make money with their art instead of having to evade police and security guards to do it. "I never really thought about my work going legal," Doze admitted. "Never in my wildest dreams did I think that painting subway trains … would lead up to galleries and museum shows."[90] Although some of their commercial work reflects their graffiti roots, many artists went in new directions. Lady Pink paints flowers, women's faces, and bar scenes on canvas; even though they are done with spray paint, they are more complex and advanced than typical graffiti-style art.

Haring was an artist who easily and quickly moved into more traditional art, partly because of his art school background. While a student at New York's School of Visual Arts in the 1970s, Haring originated a new graffiti style—chalk drawings on black paper—which he hung throughout the subway system. In 1982, when his work was exhibited at New York's Fun Gallery, Haring said he believed doing gallery work would allow people to appreciate his art more than they could have when it was illegally done in the subway system. He explained, "People who were confronted with my work could [now] take a closer and more understanding look at it and respect me as an artist."91

The newfound appreciation for graffiti allowed some artists to make a lot of money. Graffiti became especially popular in Europe. At an art auction in Paris, France, on June 6, 2007, a piece by Futura sold for $34,526 and one by JonOne sold for $36,436.

Blurred Lines

Modern graffiti burst from the nozzles of spray-paint cans. Today, however, art that adorns walls and other public spaces around the world includes work in other media, including preprinted posters. Author Nicholas Ganz believes street art is a logical extension of graffiti. In *Graffiti World: Street Art from Five Continents*, he wrote, "Letters used to dominate but today the culture has expanded: New forms are explored [and] graffiti artists have been using a wider scope of expression. [S]tickers, posters, stencils,

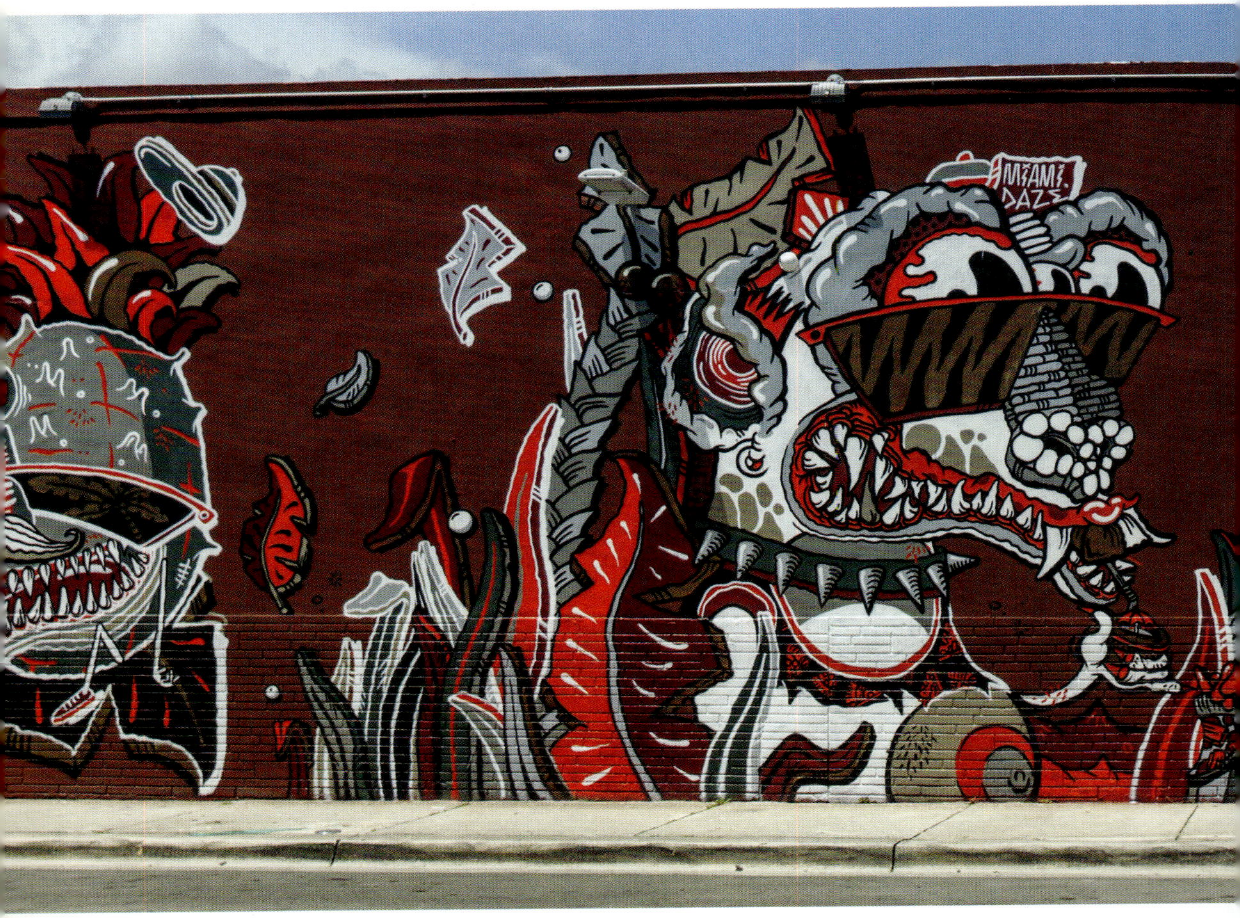

airbrush, oil-based chalk, all varieties of paint are used. Most artists have been liberated from relying solely on the spray can."[92]

Graffiti historian Cedar Lewisohn stated that it is false to make a distinction between graffiti and street art. Lewisohn defines graffiti as "any form of unofficial, unsanctioned application of a medium onto a surface" and believes that "'street art' is a sub-genre of graffiti."[93] However, of all the new graffiti forms that have evolved in recent years, the one that tests Lewisohn's flexible definition the most was created by Evan Roth and James Powderly, who founded the Graffiti Research Lab in 2006.

Roth and Powderly both have scientific backgrounds. Roth explained, "I'm not a graffiti writer. I like to say I'm a graffiti engineer."[94] Roth and Powderly use computers, laser pens, and other electronics to display graffiti at night. At the 2008 Olympic Games in Beijing, China, Powderly and four other Americans spelled out "Free Tibet" with blue LED lights near the National Stadium. They were arrested and briefly jailed for making the political statement about China's sovereignty over Tibet. The high-tech

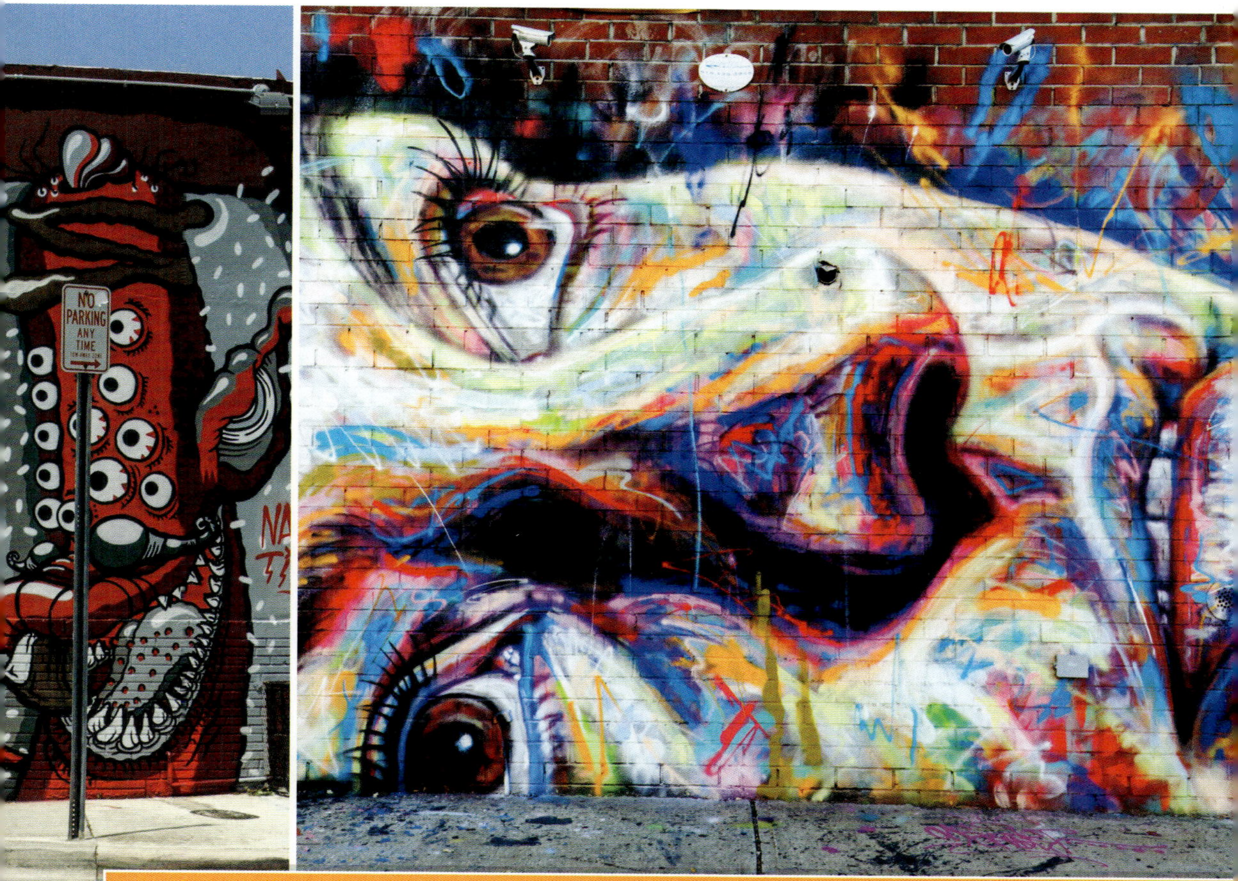

Some people see a difference between graffiti and street art; others do not.

graffiti does not permanently scar buildings, bridges, and other structures it is cast upon, and Roth and Powderly said they hope their new method will make graffiti more acceptable: "One of the goals with the Graffiti Research Lab is to try to remove some of the negative connotations that graffiti has. It's an easier pitch to sell to Mom and Dad than getting arrested every night."[95] Since LED throwies were introduced, they have grown in popularity, especially since the materials needed are inexpensive—in some places, each one can be made for under $1.

Sherm, a female graffiti artist from Los Angeles who also does graphic and web design, believes people invented new terms for graffiti because of its bad reputation. She said, "I don't know where 'street art' comes from, it seems more like a general term that the masses have come up with. Because 'graffiti' is such a bad word and has all these negative connotations attached to it still. But I've always called it graffiti because that's what my friends and all those I've known who are in this have always called it."[96]

Some people have strict definitions about what is considered graffiti versus what is considered street art. Others do not have such rigid lines but understand instinctively which types of graffiti they do and do not want to see. For example, in two suburbs of Dallas, Texas, officials had different attitudes toward two examples of graffiti found in 2017. One person had been tagging walls in the city of Richardson, Texas, with sloppy blue paint reading "J + J" and "I Luv you God & Jeana." The Richardson police posted photos on their Facebook page asking the person to stop writing this graffiti and encouraging anyone who knew the person's identity to let the police know. In contrast, when another graffiti artist painted mural-style animals on the walls of tunnels in a park in Keller, Texas, the city shared photos on its Facebook page and offered to pay the unknown artist to paint a mural in the park if they identified themselves. According to *D* magazine, which reported the story, "If you're going to graffiti property in a suburb that employs a savvy social media manager and a sense of humor, make sure you're good at it."[97]

People are much more tolerant of graffiti they feel has artistic value, such as mural-style paintings, than graffiti they see as ugly or out of place, such as simple tags on a mailbox. However, according to economist Elizabeth Currid-Halkett, "You don't have one without the other … They're both big components of graffiti subculture."[98] Additionally, sociologist Gordon Douglas noted that "if a piece is really beautiful and wheat-pasted, that doesn't mean the property owner wants it on their wall, but it probably isn't a provocation of greater disorder or a gang sign."[99]

Much of graffiti's poor reputation is due to the fact that it is illegal and often perceived to be ugly. However, many artists claim that people do not know some of the positive things that come from doing graffiti.

Should Graffiti Be Legalized?

Many people enjoy certain graffiti works and feel they are nicer to look at than a blank wall, especially one that has been badly painted by the city. These people feel rules should be put in place to help graffiti and street artists create their works legally. One suggestion is that the owners of public places should be encouraged to work with graffiti artists. This would beautify the public space and give artists a place to create their art without fear of arrest. Other countries have already embraced this strategy. For instance, in Rio de Janeiro, Brazil, "many leading street artists have put graffiti to good use for social development, founding art schools in low-income neighborhoods and partnering with the police to paint murals in run-down areas. They host large events and festivals, which bring in tourists. It has had such an effect that [in 2014,] the mayor of Rio announced the legalization of graffiti on city property that is not historical."[1]

1. Lu Olivero, "Graffiti Is a Public Good, Even As It Challenges the Law," *New York Times*, July 11, 2014. www.nytimes.com/roomfordebate/2014/07/11/when-does-graffiti-become-art/graffiti-is-a-public-good-even-as-it-challenges-the-law.

The Debate Continues

Because written graffiti is a respected part of gang culture, graffiti has helped many young men avoid joining a gang or being harassed by gang members. Gangs often respect graffiti artists, even those who are not in gangs, and leave them alone. Graffiti artist Epifanio Monarrez paints Mexican-themed murals over gang tags in Chicago as a way to "deter less well-meaning graffiti vandals while inspiring pride in the community, which has strong Mexican roots ... The gang members seem to respect his art, Monarrez said, and some even have approached him while he was painting to compliment his pieces."[100] In the 1980s, graffiti also helped Doze stay out of trouble while growing up in New York. Doze, who became a professional artist, said, "Graffiti got me on a more positive direction towards expressing myself instead of smashing a window or smashing a head."[101]

When artists talk about their craft, they always mention how hard they had to work to master graffiti. Deka, a Baltimore, Maryland, artist, said graffiti taught him the importance of having a good work ethic. Before painting graffiti, he would spend hours making and revising drawings of the pieces he created. "I would stay up crazy hours sketching," he said. "I would get a hundred page sketchbook and in a small amount of time I'd have eighty done."[102] Los Angeles artist Eklips also believes graffiti taught him positive lessons about setting goals and working hard to meet them. He said, "The best day of my life was the day my mom looked at me and she said 'I thank God for graffiti and what it's made you.' She saw that I had gained manhood and leadership through it. Graffiti [saved] my life."[103]

In recent years, graffiti has often become a positive force for cities. In London, New York, and other cities around the world, graffiti fans search for works by their favorite artists, and the money they spend in these cities is good for the economy. Additionally, art experts question whether something can be considered vandalism if a collector would pay thousands of dollars for the same piece if it were hanging in a museum. The debate about what can be considered graffiti and whether graffiti is vandalism or art will likely continue, but one thing is certain: Graffiti is here to stay.

Notes

Introduction: Understanding Graffiti

1. *Merriam-Webster Online*, s.v. "graffiti," accessed May 15, 2017. www.merriam-webster.com/dictionary/graffiti.
2. Scape Martinez, *Graff: The Art & Technique of Graffiti*. Cincinnati, OH: Impact, 2009, p. 122.
3. Stephen Powers, *The Art of Getting Over: Graffiti at the Millennium*. New York, NY: St. Martin's, 1999, p. 6.
4. Quoted in Monroe C. Beardsley, "The Faith of Graffiti," *Journal of Aesthetics & Art Criticism*, March 1975, p. 373.

Chapter One: Graffiti Through the Years

5. Bjorn Carey, "Ancient Cave Art Full of Teenage Graffiti," Live Science, February 14, 2006. www.livescience.com/7028-ancient-cave-art-full-teenage-graffiti.html.
6. Rodney S. Young, "Doodling at Gordion," *Archaeology*, October 1969, p. 271.
7. V. Pritchard, *English Medieval Graffiti*. Cambridge, UK: Cambridge University Press, 1967, p. xiii.
8. Jack Stewart, *Graffiti Kings: New York City Mass Transit Art of the 1970s*. New York, NY: Melcher Media/Abrams, 2009, p. 13.
9. "Why Gang Graffiti is Dangerous," LAPD Online. www.lapdonline.org/top_ten_most_wanted_gang_members/content_basic_view/23471.
10. Quoted in Kristen Kammerer and Bridget Snyder, *Wisdom from the Walls*. New York, NY: Boulevard, 1995, p. 11.
11. Julie Beck, "Behind the Writing on the Stalls," *The Atlantic*, November 21, 2014. www.theatlantic.com/health/archive/2014/11/behind-the-writing-on-the-stalls/383016/.

12. Wyoming State Historic Preservation Office, "The Bridger Trail: Signature Rock," Wyoming State Historic Preservation Office. wyoshpo.state.wy.us/btrail/signaturerock.html.
13. Quoted in David Fickling, "Cave Paintings Are Graffiti by Prehistoric Yobs," *Independent*, February 26, 2006. www.independent.co.uk/news/science/cave-paintings-are-graffiti-by-prehistoric-yobs-6108231.html.

Chapter Two: A New Type of Graffiti

14. Hilary Greenbaum and Dana Rubinstein, "The Origin of Spray Paint," *New York Times*, November 4, 2011. www.nytimes.com/2011/11/06/magazine/who-made-spray-paint.html.
15. Quoted in Alexandra Chalat, "What's in a Name?" *South Philly Review*, October 4, 2007. www.southwestphilly.net/view_article.php?id=6151.
16. Quoted in Stewart, *Graffiti Kings*, p. 14.
17. Quoted in Chalat, "What's in a Name?"
18. Quoted in "TAKI 183 Spawns Pen Pals," *New York Times*, July 21, 1971. graphics8.nytimes.com/packages/pdf/arts/taki183.pdf.
19. Quoted in Randy Kennedy, "Celebrating Forefather of Graffiti," *New York Times*, July 22, 2011. www.nytimes.com/2011/07/23/arts/design/early-graffiti-artist-taki-183-still-lives.html.
20. Nicholas Ganz, *Graffiti World: Street Art from Five Continents*. New York, NY: Abrams, 2009, p. 8.
21. Quoted in Dimitri Ehrlich and Gregor Ehrlich, "Graffiti in Its Own Words: Old-Timers Remember the Golden Age of the Art Movement That Actually Moved," *New York*, June 25, 2006. nymag.com/guides/summer/17406/#.
22. Herbert Kohl, *Golden Boy as Anthony Cool: A Photo Essay on Naming and Graffiti*. New York, NY: Dial, 1972, pp. 9–10.
23. Quoted in Ehrlich and Ehrlich, "Graffiti in Its Own Words."
24. David Ley and Roman Cybriwsky, "Urban Graffiti as Territorial Markers," *Annals of the Association of American Geographers*, December 1974, p. 494.
25. "What is Wildstyle Graffiti?," wiseGEEK. www.wisegeek.com/what-is-wildstyle-graffiti.htm.
26. Quoted in Jon Naar, *The Birth of Graffiti*. New York, NY: Prestel, 2007, p. 14.

27. Quoted in Kelly Bryant, "12 Things You Probably Didn't Know about Street Art," Mental Floss, February 3, 2015. mentalfloss.com/article/61441/12-things-you-probably-didnt-know-about-street-art.

Chapter Three: The Evolution of Graffiti

28. Quoted in Cedar Lewisohn, *Street Art: The Graffiti Revolution*. New York, NY: Abrams, 2008, p. 42.
29. Quoted in Edward Lucie-Smith, *American Art Now*. New York, NY: Morrow, 1985, p. 48.
30. Quoted in Cristina Verán, "Catching Wreck," *Vibe*, August 2001, p. 39.
31. Quoted in Hugo Martinez, *Graffiti NYC*. New York, NY: Prestel, 2006, p. 54.
32. Quoted in Norman Mailer, *The Faith of Graffiti*. New York, NY: HarperCollins, 2009, p. 69.
33. Quoted in Naar, *The Birth of Graffiti*, p. 12.
34. Quoted in Lucy R. Lippard, *Mixed Blessings: New Art in a Multicultural America*. New York, NY: Pantheon, 1990, p. 12.
35. Quoted in Rebecca Migdal, "Wild Style: Museum's 'Graffiti' Pays Tribute to Street 'Writers,'" *Brooklyn Paper*, June 24, 2006. www.brooklynpaper.com/stories/29/25/29_25graffiti.html.
36. Quoted in "Ket: Graffiti Artist Interview," Canned Goods, August 2009.
37. Quoted in Ehrlich and Ehrlich, "Graffiti in Its Own Words."
38. Quoted in Stewart, *Graffiti Kings*, p. 30.
39. Steve Gray, "Street Art Legends: Dondi White," Widewalls. www.widewalls.ch/street-art-legends-dondi-white/.
40. Quoted in Mailer, *The Faith of Graffiti*, p. 68.
41. Quoted in Lippard, *Mixed Blessings*, p. 165.
42. Quoted in Ehrlich and Ehrlich, "Graffiti in Its Own Words."
43. Cooper and Chalfant, *Subway Art*, p. 7.
44. Quoted in Joe Austin, *Taking the Train: How Graffiti Art Became an Urban Crisis in New York City*. New York, NY: Columbia University Press, 2001, p. 87.
45. Quoted in Lewisohn, *Street Art*, p. 30.
46. Quoted in Bryant, "12 Things You Probably Didn't Know about Street Art."
47. Quoted in Jane Fayle, "Do Female Graffiti Artists Have it Harder?," *Format*, November 5, 2016. www.format.com/magazine/features/art/female-graffiti-artists.

48. Quoted in Fayle, "Do Female Graffiti Artists Have it Harder?"
49. Quoted in Fayle, "Do Female Graffiti Artists Have it Harder?"

Chapter Four: Using Graffiti to Send a Message

50. Quoted in Colby Buzzell, "I Am Banksy," *Esquire*, December 2005, p. 198.
51. Reisner and Wechsler, *Encyclopedia of Graffiti*. New York, NY: Macmillan, 1974, p. vi.
52. Lewisohn, *Street Art*, p. 27.
53. Quoted in Silvia Viñas, "Latin American Graffiti and Urban Art: Online and in the Streets," Global Voices, June 13, 2012. globalvoices.org/2012/06/13/latin-american-graffiti-and-urban-art-online-and-in-the-streets/.
54. Adolf Hitler, *Mein Kampf*. Boston, MA: Houghton Mifflin, 1999, p. 137.
55. Holly Yan, Kristina Sgueglia, and Kylie Walker, "'Make American White Again': Hate Speech and Crimes Post-Election," CNN, last updated December 22, 2016. www.cnn.com/2016/11/10/us/post-election-hate-crimes-and-fears-trnd/.
56. Quoted in Aaron Gouveia, "Police Identify Upper Cape Graffiti Suspects," *Cape Cod Times*, February 10, 2010.
57. Quoted in Patrik Jonsson, "After Obama's Win, White Backlash Festers in US," *Christian Science Monitor*, November 17, 2008. www.csmonitor.com/USA/Politics/2008/1117/p03s01-uspo.html.
58. Gregory Locke's Facebook page, February 4, 2017. www.facebook.com/gregoryalocke/posts/1279925448727304.
59. Xavier A. Tàpies, *Street Art and the War on Terror: How the World's Best Graffiti Artist Said No to the Iraq War*. London, UK: Rebellion, 2007, p. 7.
60. Quoted in Jacqueline Maley, "24-7 Guard for Opera House," *Sydney Morning Herald*, March 19, 2003. www.smh.com.au/articles/2003/03/18/1047749748004.html.

Chapter Five: The Spread of Graffiti

61. Quoted in Nograf Network, "Graffiti Art: China's Urban Nomads Target Graffiti Canvas, the Wall," Nograf Network, December 23, 2003. nograffiti.com/grafnews/01_07_04/graffiti_art_china.htm.

62. Quoted in Cooper and Chalfant, *Subway Art*, p. 126.
63. Cooper and Chalfant, *Subway Art*, p. 124.
64. Quoted in Lewisohn, *Street Art*, p. 44.
65. Quoted in "Lyken Love: Graffiti Artist Interview," Canned Goods, September 2009.
66. Quoted in Ehrlich and Ehrlich, "Graffiti in Its Own Words."
67. "149th Street Grand Concourse," @149st, 2009. www.at149st.com/bench.html.
68. Quoted in Richard S. Christen, "Hip Hop Learning: Graffiti as an Educator of Urban Teenagers," *Educational Foundations*, Fall 2003, p. 57.
69. Quoted in Steve Grody, *Graffiti L.A.: Street Styles and Art*. New York, NY: Abrams, 2007, p. 222.
70. Sewell Chan, "A Sociologist's Look at Graffiti," *New York Times*, February 17, 2009. cityroom.blogs.nytimes.com/2009/02/17/a-new-look-at-graffiti-writers-lives/.
71. Quoted in "Os Gêmeos (The Twins)," Art Crimes, 1999. www.graffiti.org/osgemeos.
72. Quoted in Tristan Manco, Lost Art, and Caleb Neelon, *Graffiti Brasil*. New York, NY: Thames & Hudson, 2005, p. 64.
73. Quoted in "Os Gêmeos (The Twins)," Art Crimes.
74. Ganz, *Graffiti World*, p. 19.
75. Quoted in "Os Gêmeos (The Twins)," Art Crimes.
76. Quoted in Marianne Barriaux, "Graffiti Gains Ground in China," *Sydney Morning Herald*, August 21, 2009. www.smh.com.au//breaking-news-world/graffiti-gains-ground-in-china-20090821-etdv.html.
77. Lewisohn, *Street Art*, p. 9.
78. Quoted in Claudia Joseph, "Graffiti Artist Banksy Unmasked … as a Former Public Schoolboy from Middle-Class Suburbia," *Daily Mail*, July 12, 2008. www.dailymail.co.uk/femail/article-1034538/Graffiti-artist-Banksy-unmasked.html.
79. Quoted in Waldemar Januszczak, "Blek le Rat, the Man Who Gave Birth to Banksy," *Sunday Times* (London), June 8, 2008. entertainment.timesonline.co.uk/tol/arts_and_entertainment/visual_arts/article4066727.ece.
80. Eugene Volokh, "Sidewalk Chalking and the Law," *Washington Post*, May 11, 2015. www.washingtonpost.com/news/volokh-conspiracy/wp/2015/05/11/sidewalk-chalking-and-the-law/?utm_term=.fda1a8179322.

81. Quoted in "'Yarn Bomber' Hopes to Bring New Perspective to Street Art," CBS News, January 25, 2017. www.cbsnews.com/news/yarn-bombing-street-art-graffiti-london-kaye/.

Chapter Six: Is Graffiti Really Art?

82. Quoted in Glen Helfand, "The Mission School: San Francisco's Street Artists Deliver Their Neighborhood to the Art World," *San Francisco Bay Guardian*, May 24, 2002. www.sfbg.com/36/28/art_mission_school.html.
83. Quoted in Austin, *Taking the Train*, p. 80.
84. Quoted in "Vandals, Graffiti a Worry for Town," *Fiji Times*, February 18, 2009.
85. Quoted in Nograf Network, "Graffiti Art."
86. Quoted in Joel Siegel, "When TAKI Ruled Magik Kingdom," *New York Daily News*, April 9, 1989. www.zephyrgraffiti.com/otherwrt/taki183.html.
87. Lawrence Alloway, "ART," *The Nation*, September 27, 1975, p. 285.
88. Kenneth M. Lansing, "Why We Need a Definition of Art," Aristos, December 2004. www.aristos.org/aris-04/lansing1.htm.
89. Quoted in Lewisohn, *Street Art*, p. 39.
90. Quoted in "From Graffiti to Galleries," CNN, November 4, 2005. www.cnn.com/2005/US/03/21/otr.green/index.html.
91. Quoted in Lippard, *Mixed Blessings*, p. 165.
92. Ganz, *Graffiti World*, p. 7.
93. Lewisohn, *Street Art*, p. 15.
94. Quoted in Greta Dayal, "ART: Graffiti by the (Extensively Analyzed) Numbers," *New York Times*, June 25, 2006.
95. Quoted in Dayal, "ART: Graffiti by the (Extensively Analyzed) Numbers."
96. Quoted in Vincent Morgan, "Interview: Sherm," Fat Cap, December 16, 2009. www.fatcap.com/article/35.html.
97. Alex Macon, "A Tale of Two Graffiti Artists," *D*, January 24, 2017. www.dmagazine.com/arts-entertainment/2017/01/a-tale-of-two-graffiti-artists/.
98. Quoted in Shaunacy Ferro, "Can Graffiti Be Good for Cities?," Co.Design, January 27, 2014. www.fastcodesign.com/3022524/can-graffiti-be-good-for-cities.
99. Quoted in Ferro, "Can Graffiti Be Good for Cities?"

100. Karen Chen, "In Little Village, Artist Fights Graffiti with Graffiti," *Chicago Tribune*, September 8, 2013. articles.chicagotribune.com/2013-09-08/news/ct-met-little-village-graffiti-20130909_1_graffiti-art-illegal-graffiti-gang-tags.
101. Quoted in CNN, "From Graffiti to Galleries."
102. Quoted in Christen, "Hip Hop Learning," p. 56.
103. Quoted in Grody, *Graffiti L.A.*, p. 216.

For More Information

Books

Bingham, Hettie. *Banksy: Art Breaks the Rules*. London, UK: Wayland, 2016.
Although Banksy became famous through his graffiti, he has also put on exhibitions and worked on films, all while staying anonymous. This book discusses Banksy and his politically charged works.

Felisbret, Eric, and Luke Felisbret. *Graffiti New York*. New York, NY: Abrams, 2009.
This book discusses the history of the graffiti movement, supplemented by interviews with important graffiti artists as well as about 1,000 pictures.

Ganz, Nicholas, and Nancy McDonald. *Graffiti Women: Street Art from Five Continents*. New York, NY: HNA Books, 2006.
Although there are many amazing female graffiti artists, they are often overlooked in favor of male artists. This book shines a spotlight on some of the most influential female graffiti artists around the world.

Rhodes, Toni Blackwell. *The Writing on the Walls: Discovering Medieval and Ancient Graffiti for Middle School Social Studies*. Waco, TX: Prufrock Press, Inc., 2015.
Students can learn more about ancient cultures through examples of their graffiti writing and drawings.

Schacter, Rafael. *The World Atlas of Street Art and Graffiti*. Sydney, NSW: NewSouth, 2013.
This book combines large, detailed pictures with descriptions of what makes the featured works of art so special.

Websites

"The Fine Art of Yarn Bombing"

content.time.com/time/photogallery/0,29307,2077071,00.html

This *TIME* photo essay features some of the most creative yarn bombs.

Graffiti Creator

www.graffiticreator.net

Create a custom graffiti work by typing any word into the text box, then choosing colors, effects, letter width and height, and more. Users can print their creation when they are done.

Graffiti Grapher

www.csdt.rpi.edu/subcult/grafitti/index.html

This website gives a brief overview of graffiti history and allows users to create graffiti-style art on the computer using geometric concepts.

@149st

www.at149st.com

This website provides a detailed history of New York City graffiti, including a glossary of terms and photos from some of the most famous graffiti artists and crews.

Street Art Utopia

www.streetartutopia.com

This website is an online gallery of street art from around the world.

Index

Picture Credits

Cover, pp. 92–93 mariakraynova/Shutterstock.com; pp. 1, 3–4, 6, 12, 26, 38, 53, 67, 86, 97, 104, 106, 111–112 Lunarus/Shutterstock.com; pp. 7, 15, 17, 19, 29, 32, 44, 54, 63, 70, 74, 76, 81 (caption background) Jaroslav Machacek/Shutterstock.com; p. 7 (top) Pres Panayotov/Shutterstock.com; p. 7 (bottom) Jon Bilous/Shutterstock.com; p. 9 DON EMMERT/AFP/Getty Images; pp. 10, 11 A_Lesik/Shutterstock.com; p. 13 Adwo/Shutterstock.com; p. 15 Fotos593/Shutterstock.com; pp. 16–17 Naaman Abreu/Shutterstock.com; p. 17 (bottom) DeAgostini/Getty Images; pp. 18–19 (top), 93 (face) Christian Mueller/Shutterstock.com; pp. 18–19 (bottom) R.M. Nunes/Shutterstock.com; p. 21 by Ibai Acevedo/Moment/Getty Images; p. 24 KAREN BLEIER/AFP/Getty Images; p. 29 Dimitrios Kambouris/Getty Images; p. 32 Neale Cousland/Shutterstock.com; p. 33 Leonard Zhukovsky/Shutterstock.com; p. 34 dimbar76/Shutterstock.com; pp. 35, 77 meunierd/Shutterstock.com; pp. 39, 87 STAN HONDA/AFP/Getty Images; p. 40 Santiago Felipe/Getty Images; p. 42 Jemal Countess/WireImage/Getty Images; pp. 44–45 Tala-Natali/Shutterstock.com; p. 47 FRANK LEONHARDT/AFP/Getty Images; p. 50 BrooklynScribe/Shutterstock.com; p. 54 Cate Gillon/Getty Images; p. 55 Peter Turnley/Corbis/VCG via Getty Images; p. 57 Spencer Weiner/Los Angeles Times via Getty Images; p. 60 Authenticated News/Archive Photos/Getty Images; p. 61 JOHN MACDOUGALL/AFP/Getty Images; p. 63 photogeoff/Shutterstock.com; p. 66 mark higgins/Shutterstock.com; p. 69 Monkey Business Images/Shutterstock.com; pp. 70–71 Raymond Boyd/Getty Images; p. 72 Felix Lipov/Shutterstock.com; p. 74 Jeffrey Blackler/Alamy Stock Photo; p. 76 Pier Marco Tacca/Getty Images; pp. 78–79 nuu_jeed/Shutterstock.com; pp. 80–81 Alf Ribeiro/Shutterstock.com; pp. 82–83 EQRoy/Shutterstock.com; pp. 84–85 Berna Namoglu/Shutterstock.com; p. 85 (circular cover) Imladris/Shutterstock.com; p. 90 Javen/Shutterstock.com; back cover vector illustration/Shutterstock.com.

About the Author

Anna Collins lives in Buffalo, NY, with her dog, Fitzgerald, and her husband, Jason, whom she met on a road trip across the United States. She loves coffee and refuses to write without having a full pot ready.